F   Graff, Lisa
GRA   Double dog dare

Double Dog Dare

PHILOMEL BOOKS

A division of Penguin Young Readers Group.
Published by The Penguin Group. Penguin Group (USA) Inc., 375 Hudson Street,
New York, NY 10014, U.S.A. Penguin Group (Canada), 90 Eglinton Avenue East,
Suite 700, Toronto, Ontario M4P 2Y3, Canada (a division of Pearson Penguin Canada Inc.).
Penguin Books Ltd, 80 Strand, London WC2R 0RL, England. Penguin Ireland,
25 St. Stephen's Green, Dublin 2, Ireland (a division of Penguin Books Ltd).
Penguin Group (Australia), 250 Camberwell Road, Camberwell, Victoria 3124, Australia
(a division of Pearson Australia Group Pty Ltd). Penguin Books India Pvt Ltd,
11 Community Centre, Panchsheel Park, New Delhi—110 017, India. Penguin Group (NZ),
67 Apollo Drive, Rosedale, Auckland 0632, New Zealand (a division of Pearson
New Zealand Ltd). Penguin Books (South Africa) (Pty) Ltd, 24 Sturdee Avenue, Rosebank,
Johannesburg 2196, South Africa. Penguin Books Ltd,
Registered Offices: 80 Strand, London WC2R 0RL, England.

Edited by Jill Santopolo. Designed by Amy Wu.
Text set in 12.5-point Italian Old Style MT.

Library of Congress Cataloging-in-Publication Data
Graff, Lisa (Lisa Colleen), 1981– Double dog dare / Lisa Graff. p. cm.
Summary: When Kansas Bloom moves to California and joins the Media Club
at school, he soon finds himself trying to outdo one of the other fourth-grade
students in a "dare war" while vying for the job of on-air video homeroom announcer.
[1. Contests—Fiction. 2. Divorce—Fiction. 3. Moving, Household—Fiction.
4. Schools—Fiction.] I. Title. PZ7.G751577Do 2012 [Fic]—dc22 2011005721

ISBN 978-0-399-25516-8
3 5 7 9 10 8 6 4 2

Double Dog Dare

LISA GRAFF

PHILOMEL BOOKS

AN IMPRINT OF PENGUIN GROUP (USA) INC.

To Mom and Dad
and
Paula and Karl,
who have taught me so much about happiness

Contents

PROLOGUE 1

1. A PAIR OF BOYS' UNDERWEAR 13

2. A PINK CHERRY PENCIL 24

3. A VIDEO CAMERA 32

4. A FUZZY PHOTOGRAPH 39

5. A BLACK PERMANENT MARKER 48

6. A TUB OF WATER 53

7. A SECOND PAIR OF UNDERWEAR 60

8. A CRUMPLED BALL OF PINK PAPER 72

9. A TRAINED GUINEA PIG 84

10. A BASKETBALL 96

11. A BOTTLE OF GREEN HAIR DYE 104

12. A SPARKLY WHITE TUTU 106

13. A TOWERING STACK OF CDS 112

14. THREE GOLF BALLS 131

15. EIGHTY-SEVEN PACKETS OF KETCHUP 143

16. A JAR OF MUSTARD 149

17. A BAG OF JUMBO MARSHMALLOWS 169

18. A BLUE SWIVELY CHAIR. 184

19. A DIPPY BIRD. 194

20. A DESK FAN. 196

21. A SKETCHBOOK 203

22. A TENNIS BALL. 206

23. A GRANOLA BAR. 218

24. A BOUQUET OF FLOWERS 224

25. A UNICYCLE. 229

26. A HAMMER. 247

27. A PLASTIC SPOON. 252

28. A CARTON OF MILK. 263

29. AN EMPTY PLASTIC CUP 275

30. A PIECE OF CAKE 284

Double Dog Dare

PROLOGUE

Most wars begin with a bang, or a blast, or an enormous
KABOOM!

The war in room 43H began with a simple question.

"Students," Miss Sparks said to the eight members of
the Media Club gathered in her classroom that Tuesday
morning, "it's time to decide who should be the news anchor for the spring semester. Who would like to do it?"

The Media Club was not normally a place of battle.
Normally, it was a place of great cooperation, of friendship
and camaraderie. After all, the club members had a job
to do—produce and film the morning announcements,
each and every day—and they knew it was important. But

sometimes even the best of friends can have differences of opinion.

"Anyone?" Miss Sparks said. "Let's see a raise of hands."

Three hands went up—Brendan King's, Francine Halata's, and Luis Maldonado's.

"Wonderful. Brendan, why don't you tell the class why you'd like the job?"

With a grand "*Ahem,*" Brendan King rose to stand. He placed one foot on his chair, then another on his desk. And before the members of the Media Club knew what was happening, Brendan King was three feet in the air, pounding his chest with his fists and hollering, "I should be news anchor!" He shouted the words to the ceiling. "Because I'm the best in the world!"

Brendan's best friend, Andre Jackson, rose to his feet, too. "Yeah!" he hollered, not quite as loudly, but almost. "The best in the world!"

Emma Finewitz giggled.

Miss Sparks nodded calmly. She was the rare breed of teacher who didn't believe in much discipline in the

2

classroom. Miss Sparks always said that it was best to let children express themselves, that her students needed to learn to settle their own arguments in the way they saw fit. It was probably for this reason that, throughout Auden Elementary, Miss Sparks was known as the best teacher in the whole fourth grade. But she wasn't an *easy* teacher. Quite the opposite. Miss Sparks could silence an entire classroom with a single frown.

"Thank you, Brendan," she said as Brendan jumped down from his desk. "That was a very compelling argument. You may sit down now."

Brendan sat. Andre did too.

"Francine?" Miss Sparks went on. "How about you?"

Francine Halata did not climb up on her desk. Francine Halata was not a climbing-on-her-desk sort of girl. Instead, she stood, slowly, and turned to face her fellow Media Club members, tucking a strand of straw-blond hair behind her ear. "I'd really like to be the news anchor next semester," she told them. Francine had wanted to be news anchor from the very beginning of the year. As far as Francine was concerned, news anchor was the best job in the club. But when the group had voted Alicia Halladay the first news anchor, Francine hadn't complained. She'd just decided to work extra hard in her job as camerawoman to convince everyone that she should get their votes for the spring. "I need the practice, for when I'm a famous animal trainer, with my own TV show." Francine looked to her best friend, Natalie Perez, who offered an encouraging nod. "And I think I'd be really good at it. Plus, I've never missed a single day of Media Club, I'm always on time, and sometimes I stay late after school to help Miss Sparks move equipment."

Brendan mouthed something to Andre then that looked suspiciously to Francine like *teacher's pet*, but Francine soldiered on.

"So," she said, "please vote for me. Thank you." And she sat down.

"Thank *you*, Francine," Miss Sparks said. Brendan made a gagging noise, and Andre gagged, too. "Luis?" Miss Sparks continued. "Would you care to tell us why you would like to be news anchor?"

Luis shook his head. "I don't want to be news anchor," he said.

"Then why'd you raise your hand?" Alicia asked.

"Because," Luis explained, "I want to nominate someone else."

"Oh?" Miss Sparks said. She leaned back against her desk, where her dippy bird sat—its red head with its funny blue hat continually dunking its beak into a nearby glass of water for a drink.

"Yes," Luis replied. "I'd like to nominate Kansas."

Up until that point in the conversation, Kansas Bloom had been resting his head comfortably on his arms. Kansas could not care less about who got to be the news anchor. As far as Kansas was concerned, 7:05 in the morning was too early to care about anything, especially when school didn't actually start until 8:05. Kansas was the newest member of Media Club—and the newest kid at Auden Elementary, having just moved to Barstow, California, with his family the week before. He was not particularly fond of it so far.

"But—" Kansas began, but Luis cut him off.

"He's new," Luis explained, counting his reasons off on his fingers, "so it would be a good way for him to get to know the school. Plus, he's good at reading stuff, and super nice."

"And super cute!" Emma exclaimed, then immediately slapped a hand over her mouth and burst into giggles.

Kansas's face turned eggplant purple.

"He *is* pretty cute," Alicia whispered to Natalie, who nodded enthusiastically.

Francine scowled. There were more important things in life than cute boys.

"But . . ." Kansas tried again. He had only signed up for Media Club because his little sister had begged to be in Art Club, and their mother had made him pick something too, so they could take the early bus together. Kansas had begged to get out of it, but apparently he wasn't as good a beggar as his six-year-old sister. "I don't really want to be news anchor."

Brendan sneered at him. "You think you're too good for news anchor?" he said.

"Yeah," Andre said. "You think you're too good?"

"No," Kansas said carefully. "It's just—"

"What would you rather do instead?" Brendan asked.

"Yeah," Andre repeated. "What's better than news anchor?"

What Kansas *really* wanted to do was move back to Oregon, where he belonged. Where the two best friends in the world, Ricky and Will, were waiting for him. Where there was no such thing as Media Club.

Brendan and Andre were staring at him, waiting for him to answer. Everyone else seemed to be waiting, too.

"I . . ." Kansas opened his mouth, then closed it. How had he gotten in this argument? "I just . . . I don't know. Me and my friends back home, we used to do dares and stuff."

Emma's ears perked up. "Dares?"

"Yeah," Kansas told her, glad to be finally talking about something other than Media Club. "Dares."

"What kind of dares?" Natalie asked. She twirled a lock of curly brown hair around and around her finger.

Francine huffed. "I thought we were supposed to be talking about news anchor," she said. But no one seemed to hear her.

Kansas turned to Natalie. "Double dog dares," he told her. "Me and my friends Ricky and Will used to do them all the time. Like popping a wheelie on your bike while sitting backward. Or eating chili with mashed-up banana in it."

"Ooooh," Emma said. And she swooned a little bit as she said it, so that the end of the *ooooh* dipped into a sigh. "That's *so* great."

Alicia nodded in agreement, and Natalie's hair-twirling grew faster and faster.

Francine huffed again.

"No way you did that," Brendan told Kansas.

"Yeah," Andre agreed. "No way."

"Did too," Kansas replied. "I did double dog dares practically every day. Ricky and Will used to call me the King of Dares, 'cause there wasn't a single dare I wouldn't do."

When Miss Sparks clapped her hands together, the whole class snapped to attention. They had pretty much forgotten she was there.

"I think we've gotten off track," she told the students. "We were deciding who was going to be our news anchor, remember?" The eight members of Media Club nodded. "Well, then. Are there any more nominations?" The eight members of Media Club shook their heads. "Okay. Then it's time to take a vote. Everyone, please put your heads down and raise your hands when I call the name of the person you'd like to vote for."

They voted, in secrecy and silence.

When the voting was over and Miss Sparks told them they could open their eyes, there were three names written on the chalkboard, with the number of votes scrawled next to each one.

Brendan: 2

Francine: 3

Kansas: 3

"Well," Miss Sparks said, as the students took in the results. "It seems we have a tie. Francine and Kansas, would you care to split the job? It might be nice to have co-anchors at the desk for a change."

Francine did not want to split the job. She'd *earned* it. That news anchor spot should have been hers, all of it. She narrowed her eyes at Alicia, then Emma, then lastly at Natalie, three girls she'd always *thought* were her friends. One of them *must* have voted for Kansas Bloom. But which one was it?

Kansas did not want to split the job either. He hadn't joined Media Club to make a fool of himself in front of the whole school every morning. "I'd rather lick a lizard," he muttered under his breath.

"Well," Brendan said, narrowing his eyes at him, "why don't you?"

Kansas's head snapped up.

A slow stretch of a smile spread across Brendan's face. It was not a particularly friendly smile. "I double dog dare you," he told Kansas.

"*What?*" Kansas said.

"*What?*" the rest of the class exclaimed.

The smile on Brendan's face grew even more sinister. "I just think there should be some sort of tie-breaker," he said. His voice sounded friendly, but Francine, who had known Brendan for years, detected a hint of a snake in it. "Between you and Francine. So, why not a dare? Since you do them all the time and everything. Whoever does the most dares wins."

"Yeah," Andre agreed. "Whoever does the most wins."

The other members of the Media Club—turned in

unison to look at Miss Sparks. But Miss Sparks was busy erasing the names off the board. When she finished and turned around, they were still staring. Miss Sparks thought about it. "As long as you don't disrupt any other students," she said, setting down her eraser, "or violate any school rules, you are free to solve this problem in whichever way you as a group see fit." Their eyes—all sixteen of them— went wide with possibilities. "Just let me know before winter break who the news anchor will be." And she strolled to her desk, leaving the members of the Media Club to their own devices.

That was the way the war began.

By the end of first recess, Kansas had successfully completed the first dare. He'd scooped up a lizard—yellow and slimy and splotchy and *yech*—and licked it right on its scaly belly. Kansas hadn't particularly *wanted* to lick a lizard, but he'd never said no to a dare in his life, and he wasn't about to start now.

At lunch, Francine did a dare, too. She stuck a spork on her nose and balanced it there for fifteen minutes. No problem. She hadn't particularly wanted to stick a spork on her nose, but she'd been itching for that news anchor job for the past three months, and she wasn't about to lose it now.

Luis was the one who came up with the rules. One dare per kid, per day. The members of the Media Club had to vote on what each dare would be. If you completed your dare, you got a point. If you didn't, you didn't. They would keep track of the points on the chalkboard in Miss Sparks's room. Kansas's points were in the right top corner, and Francine's were in the left. Miss Sparks never mentioned anything about the points, but when she erased the chalkboard at the end of the school day, she kept the tiny white numbers in the corner: a one for Kansas, and a one for Francine.

There were fourteen school days until winter break—just under three weeks of school—which meant fourteen days of dares. Most people wouldn't think that you could cause too much chaos in just fourteen days.

Most people didn't know Francine and Kansas.

1.

A pair of boys' underwear

One.

Two.

Those were the numbers written on either side of the chalkboard in Miss Sparks's fourth-grade classroom on Thursday morning. Francine stared at them as she drummed her fingers on her desktop, waiting for Media Club to officially start. Waiting for Kansas to walk through the classroom door. He was taking *forever*.

One.

Two.

Francine had only been in this war with Kansas for two days, and already she was behind. She had one point, and Kansas had two. Yesterday, when she'd been dared to hang upside down from the monkey bars for all of second recess, the blood had rushed to her head somewhere around the eleventh minute or so, and she'd gotten dizzy and suddenly found herself—*PLOP!*—facedown on the grass with a raging headache. Kansas had been able to do *his* dare, no problem—telling the yard monitor, Mr. DuPree, that he needed to smell his armpit for a science project—so he was ahead, two points to one. But did that mean he was more worthy of being the news anchor than Francine was? No, of course not.

Francine just had to prove it.

"Francine?" Natalie asked, nudging her in the side with her elbow. "You want some pudding?"

Francine looked over at her friend, who was sitting at the desk next to her. Natalie was holding out a pudding cup from her lunch bag.

"But it's not lunch yet," Francine said. Francine's mother was morally opposed to any food that tasted good, so Natalie always shared hers. Chocolate pudding days were especially exciting. "If I eat it now, all I'll have for lunch is fava bean salad."

"Take it," Natalie said, pushing the pudding cup closer

14

to Francine's nose. She dug a plastic spoon out of her lunch bag, too. "You look like you need it."

"Thanks," Francine replied, taking the pudding and the plastic spoon. She was particularly grateful for the spoon. Natalie's mom usually packed real silverware in her daughter's lunch, but when there was chocolate pudding, Natalie always tried to sneak in a plastic spoon for Francine. That's because Francine felt strongly that chocolate pudding tasted one thousand times more delicious with a plastic spoon, instead of a metal one. She couldn't understand why everyone didn't eat it that way.

Francine peeled the foil lid off the pudding cup and licked the underside. The chocolate melted on the outside edges of her tongue, smooth and creamy and perfect. Just what she needed. "I guess I am a little jumpy," she told Natalie. Her eyes drifted to the backpack on her desk, where she was keeping her secret weapon—the thing that was going to help her defeat Kansas Bloom for sure.

Only . . . what if it didn't?

"You're really going to do it?" Natalie asked, her eyes focused on Francine's backpack, too.

Francine gulped down a mouthful of pudding, and did her best to sound confident. "Yep," she said.

"Well"—Natalie crumpled her lunch bag closed, just as Kansas strolled through the door—"good luck." And she stood up and joined the other members at the clump of desks in the corner, where they were studying that morning's newspaper.

"Thanks," Francine said, scraping out the last dregs of chocolate pudding. But she knew that real winners didn't need luck. Real winners needed courage.

When she was sure that Miss Sparks was distracted on the other side of the room, searching through her desk drawer for something, Francine made her way over to the other members of the club. With his floppy hair and ruddy cheeks, Kansas was looking cool and calm, just like the King of Dares he thought he was. Well, Francine would show him. Not even the King of Dares would do what she had planned for him.

Taking a deep breath of courage, Francine plopped her backpack dead center on the group of desks.

"What's that?" Luis asked.

"That," Francine replied, allowing herself the smallest

of smiles, "is Kansas's new dare." And, while everyone watched, Francine slowly, tooth by tooth, tugged open the zipper of her backpack. Then, with the eraser end of a number-two pencil, Francine pulled out her secret weapon and raised it from her backpack for everyone to see.

A white pair of boys' underwear, slightly used.

Emma squealed. Luis's eyes went huge, his lips round as he whistled out a "nooooooo way!" Andre snorted and thumped Kansas square on the back. "Oh, man," he said, shaking his head. "Oh, *man.*"

But Kansas was silent.

"Whose are they?" Brendan asked.

Francine paused a moment. If there was anyone in that room who should know whose tighty whities they were, it was Brendan King. After all, he'd been the one who swiped them from the boys' locker room during PE yesterday while Kansas was changing. Francine had paid him five bucks to do it. The whole dare had been his idea. But he was probably just trying to cover up so no one would suspect him of being an underwear thief.

Francine stood up a little straighter, swinging the briefs from her pencil like a pendulum. "See for yourselves," she told them. And she flung the underwear down in front of Kansas's perched elbows so that the name on the waistband was completely visible.

Kansas Bloom. The words were written in neat, square permanent marker.

Emma squealed again, so loudly that Miss Sparks popped her head up from behind her desk to see what was going on. Alicia had the sense to cover for them, fanning out the pages of the morning's newspaper and exclaiming loudly, "I cannot *believe* this thing about the strike in Greece!"

Miss Sparks went back to rummaging.

Luis inspected the briefs. "You write your name in your underwear?" he asked Kansas.

Kansas was doing his best to ignore the underwear just two inches from his left elbow. "No," he said, flicking his eyes up to meet Francine's, "I don't."

Brendan snorted. "Well, then I guess your mom does," he replied.

"What's the dare?" Alicia asked, scrunching the newspaper aside to get a closer look at the underwear.

This was it, Francine thought. This was the moment when Kansas would say, "Fine, I give up, you got me."

This was the moment when Francine would finally, officially, win the war and be declared the future news anchor of Media Club for spring semester. Just the way it should've been all along.

"I double dog dare you," she told Kansas, her stomach fluttering with the excitement of the moment. This must be how generals felt when they were about to defeat their enemies. "To string your underwear up the flagpole."

The members of the Media Club gasped. "Wow," Alicia said. "That's *good*."

"We need to vote on it," Luis reminded them, "before it's an official dare. All in favor?"

They were all in favor.

Francine turned to Kansas. She wanted to be sure to catch the exact moment when he threw his hands up in the air and quit.

But he didn't do that at all. Instead, as cool as ever, Kansas scooped his underwear off the table and said, "You want me to do it right now?"

"Wait," Francine said. "You mean you're actually going to *do* it?"

"Of course I'm going to do it," Kansas said, rolling his

eyes. Like Francine's dare was nothing to him. Like *she* was nothing. "I told you, I've never turned down a dare in my life. I'm the King of Dares."

Then he slid his chair back, the feet making an awful *thrummmmm* against the linoleum, stuffed the briefs into his back pocket, and walked across the classroom. On the way, he gave Francine a little shove, right in the shoulder. It might have been an accident. But Francine knew it wasn't.

"I can't believe he's going to do it," Natalie whispered under her breath, after the door had shut behind him. "He's so *brave*." Francine frowned at her. "Oh. But, I mean, you're totally going to win, though. Obviously." She offered her elbow to Francine, who took it after only a second's pause, and together they joined the other club members at the window, where they were already swarming for the best view of the flagpole.

The flagpole was right outside the school, next to the marquee that was currently announcing SCHOOL SPIRIT DAY TOMORROW! WEAR GREEN & WHITE! Mr. DuPree always raised the American flag in the morning right before school started—Francine had seen him do it a few times, just as Media Club was wrapping up—so at the moment, the flagpole was straight and bare, like a mast on a ship just waiting to fly its colors. One minute passed, then two. Francine did her best to breathe normally. Kansas was never going to do it, she told herself. No way.

"So what do you want to do this afternoon?" Natalie asked Francine as they waited for Kansas's floppy-haired head to pop out the main door of the school. "More guinea pig training?"

"Um . . ."

Natalie came over to Francine's house every Thursday because her dad worked late and her mom had a pottery class, and otherwise she'd have to stay with her great-aunt Mabel, who Natalie said spent most of the time sleeping in front of the TV. Natalie had been coming over every Thursday since she and Francine were in kindergarten. She knew Francine's house practically as well as Francine did—which cupboard the glasses were in, the trick to opening the laundry room door without it sticking, and the fact that the labels on the hot and cold faucets in the downstairs bathroom were switched.

Of course, Natalie hadn't come over last Thursday, because she'd had the flu. And she hadn't come over the

Thursday before that, because it was Thanksgiving. It also happened to be the Thursday that Francine's parents announced, over mashed potatoes and okra, that they were getting a divorce. Francine kept meaning to mention it to Natalie, the whole divorce thing, but it never seemed like the perfect time to tell her. Besides, the second Natalie found out that Francine's parents were getting a divorce, she was going to get freaked out and weepy and be all "oh, my gosh, Francine, you must be *so* upset!" and cry and sniffle and want to talk about it, like, nonstop. And that really didn't sound like a whole lot of fun to Francine.

"Um, yeah," Francine said. "Samson training would be great." Maybe Francine could sneak into the car before Natalie got in, and tell her mom not to mention anything. To just pretend like everything was peaches and happy and normal, like maybe Francine's dad wasn't at the house because he was off playing bridge or something. "Samson's getting sort of good at his obstacle course. He only went backward twice last time."

Beside them, Emma suddenly perked up. "I think I see him!" she squeaked.

"You do not," Brendan said, but he was leaning as far up against the window as anybody.

"Do too," Emma said. "That's him right there." She pointed.

"That's a garbage can," Alicia informed her.

"Oh, yeah."

"You guys," Francine told them, "he's not going to do it." But, like everyone else, she held her breath and waited.

2. A PINK CHERRY PENCIL

Two.

One.

Those were the numbers written on either side of the chalkboard in Miss Sparks's fourth-grade classroom. They were the last two things that caught Kansas's eye as he marched into the hallway with a pair of white boys' underwear—slightly used—in his pocket. Kansas had two points, and Francine had one. He was in the lead, and he definitely planned on staying that way. He wasn't the King of Dares for nothing.

The hallway was empty, just like it was every morning before school started. Kansas's steps echoed off the bare walls—*step, step, step*—as he made his way to the front door. He could see the empty flagpole out the window ahead of him.

And then, suddenly, he stopped dead in his tracks.

Francine had said, "I double dog dare you to string your underwear up the flagpole." *Your* underwear. But the underwear she'd given Kansas *weren't* his. Kansas had known that for a fact, as soon as he'd laid eyes on them. Because for one thing, what self-respecting fourth-grader let his mom write his name on his underwear? And for another— well, they just weren't. Francine had probably stolen them from her little brother and written the name on them herself, to try and embarrass him. Kansas didn't have a problem stringing them up the flagpole, but . . . Francine had said *your* underwear. Not *these*. She'd been trying to trick him, to make him lose a point.

Well, no way Kansas was going to fall for that. If Francine said *your* underwear up the flagpole, it was *his* underwear up the flagpole she was going to get. Kansas never failed a dare. He had the photos to prove it— pictures of every single dare he and Ricky and Will had ever done together, stuck to the wall above his bed.

Kansas quickly changed course and turned into the

25

boys' bathroom. Making sure no one was inside, he raced to the farthest stall and locked himself in. Less than one minute later, he stepped out with two pairs of underwear stuffed into his pockets, totally bare-butted under his khakis. It wasn't exactly comfortable, but he was definitely *not* going to wear some other kid's underwear.

Kansas just had one more thing to find before he was ready to do his dare. But as it turned out, that thing found him.

"*Kan*-sas! What're you doing?"

Kansas whirled around. At the far end of the hallway, by the library, was his little sister, Ginny. Her hair was pulled back into two uneven pigtails, and she still had on her ballerina tutu, the white one with the silver sparkles that she'd insisted on wearing on the early bus that morning. He'd really been hoping she'd take it off when she got to school.

"I was just looking for you," he called back, hustling over to meet her halfway. He gestured toward Mr. Benetto's classroom, where the Art Club met before school. "What're you doing out here?"

"I was going to the library," Ginny said. She was holding

a red notebook and a fat pink pencil with a red cherry eraser. "I need to look up how to spell *asthma*."

"There's a *th* in it." Kansas paused. "Why do you need to know?"

"I'm writing a note to my teacher," Ginny replied, sticking the notebook against the wall. The cherry on top of the pencil wobbled as she wrote. "I just remembered that Mom forgot to give me a note to get out of races in PE, so I'm doing it myself. Is the *th* at the beginning or the end?"

"She forgot? You sure she didn't put it in your backpack?" Ginny was always needing a note to get out of something. She had asthma—not serious, but enough that she couldn't run long distances—and she was deadly allergic to peanuts. One tiny bite, and she'd need to be raced to the hospital.

"Nuh-uh," Ginny said. "I checked. And Mom said never to call her at work unless our heads were chopped off."

"I think she meant only if it's serious."

"Well, I forgot the number anyway. Do you remember?"

Kansas frowned. "No."

"Anyway, it doesn't matter," Ginny said, still scribbling,

"'cause I'm gonna give her this one." She pulled the notebook away from the wall and flicked it into Kansas's face. "Pretty good, huh?"

> To teacher.
> Ginny has ~~azma~~ ~~azmath~~ thazma. She cant run in pe. This is her note she forgot to give you before.
>
> Mom

"Uh, Ginny, no way your teacher is going to believe Mom wrote this."

Ginny frowned. "What's wrong with it?"

"It looks like you wrote it with your feet."

Ginny grabbed the notebook back from Kansas. In one swift movement, she ripped the page out and threw it on the floor. Then she threw herself on the floor too, arms crossed and her sparkly white tutu poofed all around her.

"Maybe if you just talk to your teacher," Kansas said carefully. Ginny looked like she was going to cry. He hated when Ginny cried. Her voice got all gulpy and sniffly, and everyone always stopped what they were doing to hug her, and it took hours and was super annoying. "Maybe *I* could talk to her. Tell her that—"

"I know!" Ginny said. Her eyes were lit up, excited.

"What?"

"I'll call Dad. *He'll* tell Mrs. Goldblatt." Ginny jumped to her feet. "I'm going to the office right now."

Kansas grabbed Ginny by her tutu and dragged her back.

"Hey!"

"Ginny," he said as she tried to wiggle away from him, "you can't call Dad."

"Why not?" Ginny said, all arms and legs and squirming. She was making a ruckus, and Kansas was starting to get worried that some teacher might discover them and send them back to their rooms, and then he'd *never* get to the flagpole. "Give me one reason I can't call him."

Because, Kansas thought. *Because you've tried to call him almost every single day for the last three weeks, and he hasn't picked up once. Because last time you tried to call, the voice on the other end said the number was no longer in service. Because every time you do, you get so upset it takes a two-hour tickle fight to calm you down. Because if he really wanted to talk to us, he wouldn't have up and left in the first place.*

Kansas looked at his sister. "Because," he said, letting all the air out of his cheeks. But he couldn't say it. He couldn't say any of it. She was only six, for crying out loud. He shook his head, and then gently took the notebook from her. "Because *I'm* going to write you a note," he said, and he smoothed his hand across a fresh sheet to think.

Ginny clapped her hands together. "Oh, good!" she said. She handed Kansas the cherry pencil. "Thanks, Kansas. You're smart."

Kansas studied the blank page and thought. Then, when he had it all figured out, he put the pencil to the paper and began to write.

The good thing about growing up with a mom who worked late all the time and a dad who was usually who-knew-where was that you got really good at forging letters. Need a parent to sign off on your C-spelling test? Mom forgot to look at that permission slip before she raced out the door? Kansas was your guy. He had his mother's hand-writing down perfectly—from the loopy *S* in Susie to the jutting curve of the *m* in Bloom.

When he was finished, Kansas signed the note with a practiced flourish and passed it to Ginny to inspect.

> *Dear Mrs. Goldblatt,*
> *My daughter, Virginia Bloom, has asthma and will not be able to do any races for the rest of the year.*
> > *Sincerely,*
> > *Susie Bloom*

He was especially proud of the *Sincerely.* He'd memorized that word about a year ago, just in case.

"This is perfect!" Ginny cried, clutching the note to her chest. "Thanks, Kansas!" And she left a wet kiss on his cheek.

"No problem," he told her, wiping his cheek clean. He handed her back the pink cherry pencil. "Now I need you to help *me*."

3.

A video camera

Brendan and Alicia had wrenched one of the windows open, and a waft of early-morning air—sweet and crisp and full of that barely-December sting that Francine loved so much—was breezing across Francine's face. She had stood, with the members of the Media Club, watching, for three minutes, then four, but so far Kansas had not appeared at the flagpole. The clock ticked away.

"Do you think he chickened up?" Emma asked, standing on her tiptoes to lean farther out the window.

"Huh?" Luis asked.

"She means chickened out," Alicia explained.

"Oh."

Francine checked the clock again.

"Where do you think he is?" Natalie asked.

Brendan snorted. "Maybe he got so scared he fainted. Maybe he's in the nurse's office right now." He turned his back to the window. "The King of Dares, *ha*! What a baby."

"Yeah," Andre agreed, turning his back to the window, too. "What a baby!"

Francine tried not to let herself smile at that. She wouldn't be smug when she beat Kansas, she decided. She'd very politely shake his hand and tell him that he'd put up an excellent fight.

"Let's give him until the bell rings," Luis said. "If his underwear's not up by then, he doesn't get the point. Everyone agree?"

Everyone did. They turned back to the window to watch and wait.

"Everything okay over here?"

Seven heads whirled around from the window. Miss Sparks was standing behind them, arms across her chest. "You all seem a little . . . preoccupied," she said, a smirk of a smile on her face. "Is there something that's disrupting our club time?"

They shushed and coughed, all of them, poking one another in the sides and clearing their throats, and generally acting—Francine thought—like a bunch of criminals caught in the middle of a bank heist.

"Oh, um, we're fine," Alicia said quickly. "Just checking to see if the weather forecast is right."

Miss Sparks nodded in that knowing way she had. "I see," she replied. "Well, now that you're sure it is indeed cloudy, perhaps we should begin getting ready for today's announcements, don't you think? Only thirty minutes until the bell rings. Francine, can you give me a hand with the extension cord for the camera?"

And that was that. They all went about their business, same as they did every morning. But they left the window open, and Francine noticed that she wasn't the only one whose eyes kept darting to the flagpole, tall and sturdy and completely flagless.

As Francine helped unroll the orange extension cord and cover it with the heavy gray mat so no one would trip on it, she snuck in a quick whisper to Natalie.

"No way Kansas'll do it," she said. She was growing more and more positive by the second. "And even if he *does* do it, he'll get in trouble, and then no way he'll get to be news anchor. Mrs. Weinmore will kick him out of the club for sure." Mrs. Weinmore, Auden Elementary's principal, was famous for her harsh punishments.

Natalie frowned. "Don't you think you might get in trouble too, if Mrs. Weinmore finds out you're the one who dared him?"

Francine tugged at a knot in the extension cord. "No way. Anyway, it was Brendan's idea, not mine."

"Just be careful, okay?" Natalie replied. "Otherwise you'll *both* get kicked out, and then who would be news anchor?" And she crossed the room to help Alicia get ready.

Francine shot another quick look out the window. Still no Kansas. Still no underwear.

The last half of Media Club passed quickly, just as it always did. While Francine did her special duties as camerawoman—unlocking the camera from the closet, setting it up at the front of the classroom, checking all the settings—the other members had their own tasks to perform. Alicia, the news announcer for fall semester, was the star of the show. She set herself up behind Miss Sparks's desk, in the large swively chair right behind Miss

Sparks's red dippy bird, and studied the morning's announcements while Natalie, who was in charge of hair and wardrobe, made sure that she was "camera ready," occasionally dabbing at her face with a tissue.

Brendan was the news editor, so he was in charge of setting the order of everything Alicia read each morning, deleting any duplicates, and adding in any last-minute announcements. Those came from Luis and Kansas, the show's runners, whose job it was to race around to all the classrooms before the bell rang and collect any new announcements the teachers might have.

Just fifteen minutes to go.

There was a tremendous crash from Francine's right. Emma had managed to knock over an entire stand of lights. Emma was the "special effects technician," which, as far as Francine could figure out, simply meant that she had to make sure everything was plugged into the wall. It wasn't a difficult job, but somehow Emma still found a way to make it challenging.

"Oh, man!" Andre called. Andre was in charge of lighting. "One of the bulbs broke!"

Miss Sparks scuttled over to help clean up the mess. "Andre," she said calmly, "go ask Mr. Paulsen if there's an extra bulb in the drama room we can borrow." And Andre scurried out of the room, shooting angry eyes at Emma as he went.

Francine tried to relax, settling herself behind the camera. This was always her favorite part of the morning—just before the rest of her classmates showed up and filed into their seats behind her, in those last few minutes of calm before the bell rang and everything became whisper-quiet all across the school. Everything, that is, except Alicia's voice as she told the entire school the announcements of the day, courtesy of Francine and her news camera.

And Francine was just letting that warm, fresh, happiness envelop her, when—with only eight minutes left until the bell rang—she heard Emma's piercing squeal.

"What?" Brendan asked. "What did you break this time?"

But Emma didn't answer. One hand was clamped over her mouth, and the other was pointing out the window.

From where she was standing in front of Miss Sparks's

desk, Francine had to squint to see it. But she could just make it out—Kansas, standing in front of the flagpole, grinning like an idiot, like he was about to get his picture taken or something. And high atop the flagpole above him, something small and white was swaying in the December breeze.

Francine had never been quite so depressed to see a pair of underwear.

4. A FUZZY PHOTOGRAPH

"Take the picture!" Kansas called to Ginny. She was standing in front of the school marquee, blocking parts of the words SCHOOL SPIRIT DAY TOMORROW! WEAR GREEN & WHITE! so that all Kansas could see, around her tutu, was SCHOOL MORROW! WE ITE!

It hadn't been too hard to string his underwear up the flagpole once they'd finally gotten outside. The flagpole was still flagless, so all Kansas had to do was grab the rope, clip the briefs on, and haul them up.

The hard part was getting Ginny to snap a photo before anyone saw them. Kansas hadn't read Auden Elementary's official rule book or anything, but he was pretty sure that stringing a pair of underwear up the flagpole would *not* be considered acceptable behavior.

"You just push the big button!" he shouted.

Ginny wasn't the greatest photographer, but she'd have to do, since Ricky and Will were back in Oregon. Ginny had taken a photo of the dare he'd done yesterday too— telling Mr. DuPree that he needed to smell his armpit for a science project—and that one had turned out okay. Kansas hadn't gotten a photo of the lizard-licking dare on Tuesday, which was too bad, because that was pretty much the grossest dare Kansas had ever done. But Ginny had helped him re-create it when they got home, with a lizard from their backyard that Kansas pretend-licked for the camera. It wasn't quite the same, but it would do for the Wall of Dares in his bedroom, and he knew Ricky and Will would get a kick out of it when they finally checked their e-mails. Now, Kansas was always prepared—carrying around the cheap digital camera his dad had given him in his back pocket at all times.

Ginny snapped the picture.

Kansas hustled Ginny back to Art Club with—he

checked the clock on the wall of the art room—twelve minutes until the bell rang. Kids were already starting to trickle into the hallway, and he could hear a few murmurs here and there that sounded quite a bit like "flagpole" and "underwear."

Kansas was just making his way back to Media Club when he noticed Luis heading out of a classroom two doors away, a stack of papers in his hands.

"Hey, Kansas!" Luis called, stopping so that Kansas had no choice but to talk to him while they walked together.

"Hey," Kansas said. He was still the tiniest bit mad at Luis for nominating him for news anchor.

Luis grinned at him. "Did you do the dare?"

At that, Kansas couldn't help but grin back. He pulled the camera out of his back pocket to show him, flipping the On switch as they continued down the hallway. But his grin quickly faded. "Aw, man! Ginny cut my head off!" He brought the camera close to his nose. All you could see was the tip-top of Kansas's hair, poking out in front of the flagpole.

Luis leaned in to look. "At least she got the underwear, though," he said. "That's really the important part."

"I guess," Kansas grumbled. The entire image was fuzzy, completely out of focus.

"If you want someone to take pictures for you, you know, I could do it. I took a photography class this summer. I'll bring my camera tomorrow. It's one of the old-fashioned ones. You know, like, with film?"

"Um," Kansas said. People actually had those still? "Thanks. That'd be cool."

"No problem." Luis was riffling through the papers in his arms, last-minute announcements from various teachers. "Hey," he said, "are you going to be around over winter break?"

"Nah. I'm going camping with Ricky and Will. We go every year with Ricky's dad, out in Glenyan, for, like, three days. We go rock climbing and ride ATVs, and Ricky's dog comes too. It's freezing, but it's awesome." He tried to return his camera to his back pocket, but it was too stuffed in there with the underwear. He put it in his front pocket instead. "How come?"

Luis shrugged. "Nothing. It's just my birthday party.

I was going to invite you, if you were around. It's all Marvel."

"Marvel?"

"Yeah. Like the comic books? Spider-Man, X-Men, the Hulk . . ."

"Oh." That sounded okay, Kansas thought, but not as fun as camping. "Well, too bad I have to miss it."

Just as they were about to reach Miss Sparks's door, Kansas was bumped from behind, hard. He turned around.

It was Andre Jackson, holding a box of lightbulbs. "Look where you're going, doofus," he told Kansas. But he was grinning when he said it, and Kansas was pretty sure he'd bumped into him on purpose. Kansas shook his head and opened the door to room 43H.

What Kansas *planned* on doing, when he stepped into the room, was to pull the underwear out of his pocket, the fake *Kansas Bloom*s, and shove them right in Francine's face, and tell her, "You can't get me that easy, Francine!" And then he'd make her add his third point to the board herself.

But he didn't do that, for two reasons.

The first reason was that Francine Halata was already standing at the chalkboard, changing his two to a three.

And the second reason was that the underwear—the ones with *Kansas Bloom* written across the waistband—were no longer in Kansas's pocket.

Somewhere, between the flagpole and his classroom, Kansas had lost them.

Kansas wriggled in the hard wooden library chair. It wasn't a comfortable chair to begin with, and the fact that there was nothing but a thin pair of khakis between it and his buttocks wasn't helping matters. Kansas was pretty sure that by the end of the day, his butt was going to be chafing big time. But sometimes that was the price you had to pay to be the King of Dares.

Kansas held his breath as he logged into his e-mail account. And then, he let it out. Finally. An e-mail from Will.

FROM: Tiger44

TO: ksrocks

hey dude! thx 4 the pix. ricky sayz he doesn't think that lizard 1 is real tho. NEway glad u like ur new school so much. ricky found a 3rd kid for

44

**camping, mark h. remember him? too bad you
had to move.**

miss you!

later, w.

Kansas felt his stomach sink to his feet. Mark H.? *Mark H.* was going camping? Ricky and Will hadn't even *asked* Kansas if he wanted to go. Like he suddenly wouldn't like camping anymore, just because he'd moved away.

Kansas felt like a moron. He should've told Ricky he still wanted to go this year. He should've made sure they knew.

But they hadn't even *asked* him.

Kansas logged into his IM account. If Ricky or Will was on right now, he could talk some sense into them. It would be faster than e-mail. He typed in his username, kansas_ the_champ, and his password, and opened up his "friends" box. But neither Ricky nor Will was online. They were probably at lunch, hanging out with their new best friend, Mark H.

"Hey, Kansas!"

Kansas jumped with a start. It was Brendan, leaning

45

against the back of his chair, peering over his shoulder at the computer. Next to him was Andre, peering over Kansas's shoulder too.

"Oh," Kansas said. "Hey." He logged out of his e-mail and IM with two quick clicks of the mouse, then turned around in his chair. "What's up?"

"It took us forever to find you," Brendan said. "What are you doing in the library during *lunch*?"

"Yeah," Andre agreed. "Why are you in the library?"

Kansas shrugged. "Checking e-mail."

"Well, we were looking for you because we thought of a dare for Francine," Brendan said. "Everyone's voted on it but you, and they all think it's awesome."

"Yeah," Andre said. "Awesome."

"What is it?"

"She has to go inside the boys' bathroom," Brendan said, "and write *Francine was here* on the wall."

"Won't she get in trouble?" Kansas asked. "I mean, if someone finds out?"

"Yeah, probably," Brendan said. "But you probably would've gotten in trouble for the flagpole thing if you got

46

caught, and Francine didn't seem to care about you. So come on. You vote yes or what?"

"Yeah," Andre said. "Or what?"

Kansas thought about it. "Sure," he told Brendan. "I vote yes."

"Cool. We gotta make her do it before lunch is over. You should come with us." And Brendan walked toward the door, snatching a thick black marker off the librarian's desk as he went. Andre walked right behind him.

Kansas thought, but he wasn't certain, that he could just make out a suspicious bulge in the back pocket of Andre's jeans—a bulge that looked a whole heck of a lot like a wadded-up pair of underwear. He even thought he maybe saw the hint of a waistband sticking out, with what might just be the letter K on it. But Kansas didn't say anything about it. What was he supposed to say? "Hey, Andre! Do you have a pair of underwear with my name on them in your pocket?" Uh, no. So, without another word about anything, Kansas followed Brendan and Andre out of the library to find Francine.

5.

A black
permanent marker

Not that Francine had ever spent any time thinking about
it, but if she had, she would have assumed that a boys'
bathroom would smell pretty similar to a girls' bathroom—
soap and floor cleaner and just a little of that classic bathroom stink.

It did not. The boys' bathroom smelled quite a bit like
the inside of one of her dad's gym socks. She could smell it
even from the hallway, with the door partially open.

Kansas finished checking underneath the last stall door
for feet and gave Francine the all clear. Andre held the
door open for her, then handed her the black permanent
marker. Brendan grinned his sinister grin. "Good luck,"
he told her. But Francine could tell he didn't really mean it.

"Don't worry," Natalie assured her. "If any boys are about to come in, I'll pound on the door so you can hide."

"Thanks," Francine said with a gulp. The last thing she wanted to see that afternoon was *boys peeing*. She stepped inside, and the door shut firmly behind her.

Francine uncapped the marker and looked around for a good place to write her message. She didn't want to do it anyplace obvious, where the janitor would see it and she'd get in trouble.

A faucet dripped.

Settling on the tile wall beneath the sink, Francine crouched down, head below a rusty pipe, and began to scribble.

Francine was here

She'd just finished the last letter when she heard it.

Pound, pound, pound.

Natalie was knocking on the door! Francine's head shot up—*smack!*—into the bathroom sink. "Ouch!" she cried, then slapped a hand over her mouth. This was no time for sissies.

Tossing the marker quickly in the garbage can, Francine raced to the farthest stall against the wall and locked herself inside. Then she stood up on the rim of the toilet bowl, crouching slightly so her head wouldn't show over the door. She could hear the main door to the bathroom creak open. Francine hoped that whoever had come in would pee and leave quickly. She didn't want to spend one more second in that nasty stall than she had to.

But the person did not pee. The person shouted.

"Francine Halata!"

Francine's legs began to tremble underneath her. The voice on the other side of the door was unmistakable. It belonged to none other than Mrs. Weinmore, Auden Elementary's bulldog of a principal.

"Francine HALATA!"

That fink Kansas had tricked her, Francine realized. He and Brendan and Andre must've raced for the principal the second she walked through the bathroom door. That was probably their plan all along.

"I know you're in here, Miss Halata!"

Maybe, Francine thought, if she could stay perfectly quiet, she'd be okay. Mrs. Weinmore wouldn't know for sure she was in the boys' bathroom unless she saw her. Even if she suspected, she'd never be able to prove—

Ka-POP! The stall closest to the door was swung open, then the next one. *Ka-WHACK!* Mrs. Weinmore was making her way down the row, checking inside every one. *Ka-FLING! Ka-THUD! Ka—*

"Miss Halata!" The door of the stall Francine was hiding inside began to shake, the lock banging against the frame. "You come out of there this instant!"

Francine's legs trembled more wildly on top of the toilet seat, and her head was throbbing so badly she thought her brain might burst from her skull. Still, she remained silent. Mrs. Weinmore could jiggle that door all she wanted. Francine was *never* coming out. She'd stay there all night if she had to. All week. Sooner or later, Mrs. Weinmore would have to go home, and until then, Francine would just—

SPLASH!

Before Francine knew what had happened, her trembling legs had quivered right out from underneath her, and she found herself tumbled onto the bathroom floor, flat on her back, with one foot ankle-deep in toilet water.

But worse than any of that was the sight of Mrs.

Weinmore's beet-red face, glaring at her from underneath the stall door.

"Oh, um, hey, Mrs. Weinmore," Francine said as casually as she could manage, as if she hung out with her feet in toilets every day. Francine could feel the toilet water seeping through her sock. "Fancy meeting you here."

Mrs. Weinmore did not look amused.

6. A TUB OF WATER

As soon as Francine stepped inside the bathroom, Brendan raced off down the hall. Andre kept checking his watch, looking as excited as Ginny did on Christmas morning, but Kansas couldn't figure out what was so great about hanging out outside a boys' bathroom. Francine had only been inside for twenty seconds, and already he was bored.

Andre leaned in close to Kansas, jerking his head toward Natalie. "Hey, you think Brendan needs help?" he whispered. "What if Mrs. W.'s not in her office?"

"Huh?" Kansas replied. He had no idea what Andre was talking about. He was more worried about stupid Mark H., and whether or not Ricky's dad would let him drive one of the ATVs by himself. Probably. Probably Mark H. was the best ATV driver in the whole world.

"I'm gonna go help," Andre decided, checking his watch again. "You wait here, in case Brendan comes back."

"Comes back from where?" Kansas asked. But Andre didn't answer. He was already ten feet down the hallway.

"Hey, Kansas," he called, whirling around with a smile on his face, "check out the dingbat with the tutu!" He pointed as he continued down the hallway.

Tutu?

Kansas squinted. Sure enough, there was Ginny at the far end of the hall, sitting on the floor outside her classroom. In her tutu. And she was *crying.*

"She's my little sister," Kansas told Andre as he raced past him down the hallway. "And she's not a dingbat!" Actually, Kansas thought as he ran, Ginny *was* a dingbat. Like, 95 percent of the time. But only Kansas was allowed to think that, because he was her brother.

"Ginny!" Kansas said when he reached her. She was slouched against the wall, her tutu flared around her, and she didn't look up, just kept her face buried in her hands. Kansas wanted to tell her to stop being such a baby, that she was causing a scene in the middle of the hallway and it was making them both look seriously uncool. He wanted to pick her up under the armpits and stuff her and that stupid tutu back into her first-grade classroom.

But she was *crying,* for Pete's sake.

Glancing around to be sure that no one he knew was watching, Kansas crouched down next to her. "What happened?" he asked.

Ginny lifted her face from her tutu, little bubbles of snot coming out of her nose. "She said it wasn't real," she told him.

Kansas sighed. "Who said what wasn't real?" he asked.

"The note." She let out a tiny sniffle. "Mrs. Goldblatt said she knew that Mom didn't really write it." Sniffle.

"Is that all?" Kansas said. He put his arm around his sister and gave her a little squeeze. "Ginny, don't even worry about it. I'll fix it, all right?" Next to Ginny's classroom door, a leak from the ceiling was dripping down into a tub of murky water. *Drip. Drip.* "I'll just go talk to your teacher and tell her that our mom works, like, all the time, so she couldn't—"

"No-*oooo,*" Ginny wailed. "That's not . . ." She began

gulping down air, huge chunks of it, and Kansas knew that if he couldn't calm her down soon, she'd be leakier than the ceiling in two seconds flat, a tutu-wearing tear machine. "She said she knew 'cause of the name."

"What are you talking about?" Kansas said, eyes darting around to see who was watching them. There were a few third-graders peering at them from over by the gym, but so far that was it. Andre had completely disappeared. But Kansas didn't have time to wonder about that, because Ginny was wailing again.

"*Mom's* name," she said. She sniffled in time with the drips in the bucket—*sniffle, drip, sniffle, drip.* "'Cause you wrote Susie Bloom."

"What else would I write?"

"Mrs. Goldblatt said now Mom's using her *maiden* name. That now she's Susie"—*sniffle, drip*—"Cheever."

"What? Cheever?"

"Yeah." *Sniffle, drip.* "That was her last name 'fore she married Dad."

"I *know* it was her . . . Are you sure?"

Ginny went back to weeping into her tutu. "You think it's true, Kansas?" she said, peeking an eye out of her ruffles.

Sniffle, drip.

"Yeah," Kansas said with a sigh. "I guess it's probably true."

Sniffle, drip.

"But then . . . Kansas?"

"Yeah?"

"Does that mean *we* gotta be Cheevers?"

"Huh?" Kansas hadn't thought of that before.

"Cheever-Cleaver. Cheever-Cheetoh. Cheever-Cheetah. Blech. I don't like it."

"Me neither," he said. "But I don't think we have to change if we don't want to."

"Good."

"You should get back to class, probably."

"Mrs. Goldblatt made me come out here 'cause she said I was hysterical," Ginny said, wiping her tears off her face with the back of her hand.

"Mrs. Goldblatt sounds like a cow," Kansas replied.

Ginny giggled.

"Come on," Kansas told her, hoisting himself to his feet. He held out a hand to help Ginny up too. "I'll talk to her and explain about the note, okay?"

"'Kay. But . . . Kansas?"

He sighed again, hand on the doorknob to Ginny's classroom. "Yeah?"

Ginny shifted her weight to her right foot, then her left. "Dad's coming back, though, right?" she said. She looked up at Kansas. "Right?"

Kansas blinked.

There weren't too many things that Kansas knew for certain. He wasn't good at geography, he had to think super hard every time he did division, and he could barely spell to save his life. But he did know *one* thing for absolutely positive, and that was that their dad was never coming back for good. He'd left before, three years ago, when Kansas was just Ginny's age. And for a whole month Kansas had waited and hoped and hoped and waited for him to come back, even though his mom had tried to tell him a billion times it wouldn't happen. But then it *did* happen, just the way Kansas had been hoping for. Ginny had gotten sick and had been raced to the hospital the day they discovered her peanut allergy, and their dad had come racing, too, not far behind. At the time, Kansas had thought it was some sort of miracle.

Now, of course, Kansas knew that his dad coming back hadn't been a miracle. A miracle would've been his dad staying away forever. Now things were going to be better. His mom was getting a divorce, official and everything. He'd overheard her telling his aunt Grace on the phone. And he knew, he *knew,* that his dad was never coming back to stay. And that was the very best thing.

But try telling a six-year-old that.

"I don't know," he told Ginny at last.

She smiled at him as she slipped her hand into his. "Don't worry, Kansas," she said. "He will." Then she twisted open the doorknob and stepped back inside her class, face as clear as though nothing had ever upset her at all.

7.

A second pair of underwear

Francine sat in the hard wooden chair in front of Mrs. Weinmore's desk, her toes squishing inside her wet sock. The principal was staring at her over thick-rimmed glasses, like she was a cop in one of those police shows Francine's dad was always watching, and she was waiting for a full-blown confession. Which was pretty stupid, Francine thought, because she'd been caught lying on the floor of the boys' bathroom with her foot in a toilet, so really, what else was there?

"Can I go back to class now?" Francine asked. The bell had rung five minutes ago, and yet here Francine sat.

"Not yet," Mrs. Weinmore replied.

"Oh."

Mrs. Weinmore sucked in her cheeks as she studied Francine, and then she picked a piece of lint off of her peach blazer. Francine's mother would have said that peach was not a flattering color for Mrs. Weinmore's complexion, but Francine figured maybe she should keep that information to herself.

Francine waited as one minute ticked by on the clock above Mrs. Weinmore's desk. Then two.

"Can I go back to class *now*?" she asked.

Mrs. Weinmore frowned at her. Francine took that as a no.

"Miss Halata," the principal said at last, and she took such a deep breath after she said it that Francine began to wonder if that was the first breath she'd taken since they'd been sitting there. She let out all her air. "Miss Halata," she said again.

"Um . . . yes?"

Mrs. Weinmore did not respond.

Francine went back to looking at the clock. Maybe this was her punishment—sitting in a hard wooden chair, watching the clock tick away the minutes until the end of time. It was a pretty good one.

"Quite frankly, Miss Halata," Mrs. Weinmore piped up at last, "I'm concerned about your behavior." She set her elbows on the table and leaned forward to look at Francine more closely. "I find it rather bothersome."

Francine snapped her attention away from the clock. "Um, bothersome?"

"Yes. Bothersome. You've been attending Auden Elementary since kindergarten, Miss Halata. Five long years. And I like to think that in that time we've gotten to know each other pretty well. Wouldn't you say that we know each other pretty well?"

"Um . . ." Was this a trick question? Was Mrs. Weinmore going to quiz her on her favorite color? What if Francine got it wrong? "Um, yeah," she replied. "Sure."

"I think so too. And that's why I find your behavior this afternoon to be so out of character. Not like the Francine Halata I've always known. Which makes me think"—she twitched her bulb of a nose thoughtfully—"that there might be something else going on with you."

Francine's stomach thunked, heavy like a rock, right to the bottom of her innards. "Um . . . going on?" she said.

Mrs. Weinmore folded her hands under her chin. "Yes,"

she said. "I think you've been acting differently ever since the Thanksgiving break. Am I right?" Francine didn't move a muscle. "And I think I know why."

Francine could feel the back of her neck burning. If her parents were getting a divorce, it was none of Mrs. Weinmore's beeswax. "I don't want to talk about it," she grumbled.

Mrs. Weinmore nodded at that. "Well, perhaps you don't," she replied. "But I think it's worth discussing. You know, dear, your situation is not uncommon."

"It's . . . it's not?" Francine had heard that, that lots of kids' parents got divorces. But she didn't know any.

"Oh, no, not at all. As principal, I see it all the time. And it's nothing to be concerned about. It's perfectly normal for a girl your age."

Francine raised an eyebrow.

"The important thing," Mrs. Weinmore continued, "is not to forget who you are, dear, simply because you've fallen in love."

Francine nearly toppled out of her chair. "In *love*?" she squeaked.

Mrs. Weinmore nodded again. "Infatuation, attraction,

puppy love. I've seen it a thousand times before. A young girl develops a crush on a boy and loses herself trying to win his affections." She adjusted the glasses on her nose. "It's a hopeless game, dear. I wouldn't advise it."

Francine was pretty sure Mrs. Weinmore had lost her marbles. "B-but . . . ," she sputtered, "I'm not . . . who . . . ?" She righted herself in her seat. "Mrs. Weinmore," she said, "I don't know what you're talking about. I don't have a crush on anyone."

"I hate to argue with you," Mrs. Weinmore replied. "But the evidence seems clear."

"Huh?"

"Wouldn't you agree," Mrs. Weinmore went on, "that it seems an awfully big coincidence that your sudden shift in personality occurred at the exact same time as the arrival of a certain someone—a certain *boy*—at Auden Elementary?" She leaned forward just an inch. *"Hmmm?"*

Kansas Bloom? The principal thought Francine had a crush on *Kansas Bloom?* Francine squeezed her eyes shut. She was pretty sure her brain was going to explode.

"Miss Halata?"

Francine opened her eyes. "I do *not* like Kansas," she told the principal.

"I see," Mrs. Weinmore replied. "Then maybe you would care to explain why a little birdie informed me that you paid five dollars to collect these"—she pulled open one of her bottom desk drawers—"underpants from the boys' locker room yesterday?" Mrs. Weinmore slapped the underwear on her desk. They were the same pair of briefs Francine had been carrying in her backpack just that morning—white, slightly used, with the name Kansas Bloom written on the waistband in square black letters.

"Is that why you were peeping in the boys' room, dear?" Mrs. Weinmore went on. "So you could see your little friend?"

"What?" Francine cried. "No!" This could *not* be happening. Her mind raced, trying to grab at the words that would get her in the least amount of trouble. "I'm not— I didn't— Those are the underwear Kansas put up the flagpole this morning," she said at last. "He should be the one in trouble, not me."

Mrs. Weinmore sighed, as though Francine had said

the exact wrong string of sentences. "Is that so?" she asked.

"Um . . . yes?"

"Interesting," the principal replied, in a tone of voice that let Francine know that she didn't think it was interesting in the slightest. "It's interesting you say that, Miss Halata, because I was hoping to trust you here. But it just so happens that these *weren't* the underpants that were up the flagpole this morning."

"Yes, they were," Francine said. She really wished Mrs. Weinmore would stop saying "underpants." "Kansas put them there, he did. I swea—"

"No. He didn't. You know it, Miss Halata, and I know it. These underpants were not the ones on the flagpole." She opened up her desk drawer again and pulled something else out. "*These* were." And she set the object on the desk between them.

It was a white pair of boys' underwear, slightly used. A second pair.

How many pairs of underwear did Mrs. Weinmore have in there?

"Now," Mrs. Weinmore said, "I'm going to ask you one

last time, and I expect you to tell me the truth. Did you or did you not pay five dollars to acquire a pair of Mr. Bloom's underpants?"

"But—" Francine began. She was so confused. If Kansas hadn't put his underwear up the flagpole, then who had? "But . . ."

"Miss Halata, the truth, please."

Francine sighed. "Yes," she said at last. "I did."

Mrs. Weinmore studied Francine's face for a long moment, then finally opened up her bottom desk drawer and dropped both pairs of underwear inside. "Very well," she said. "Normally I would call a student's parents to report such a stunt. Normally I would say you wouldn't be allowed to participate in any extracurriculars for the rest of the school year." Francine gulped. Was she being kicked out of Media Club? "But given the circumstances surrounding the situation, I'm going to let you off the hook."

Francine felt as though her legs were covered in tiny prickles of fire ants. "Can I go now?" she asked. The only thing she wanted in the world was to get out of that chair and leave.

"Yes," Mrs. Weinmore said. "But take this as your

warning. The next time you misbehave, I promise you I won't be so lenient."

"Thanks," Francine said, leaping to her feet. "I'll remember."

"Miss Halata?"

Francine whirled around, already halfway out the door. "Yeah?"

"I've found that boys tend to like you best when you act like the person you truly are inside." She winked.

Francine hustled out the door.

When Francine got back to class, the first thing she saw were the numbers on the chalkboard. Kansas had three points, same as that morning, and Francine had two.

"Sorry I'm late," she told Miss Sparks, handing over her pass. "I had to, um, talk to Mrs. Weinmore about something."

"Thanks," Miss Sparks said. "Oh, and Francine?" She held out a thin pink square of paper, the kind the office secretary used to record messages. "This came for you while you were at lunch." Francine took it and headed back to her desk.

The thing Francine couldn't figure out was how Mrs. Weinmore knew about her buying Kansas's underwear. Brendan had to have been the one to tell her, because he was the only person who knew about it. But why would he do that, if he was the one who stole them?

There was a note poking out from the front of Francine's desk, and Francine knew it must be from Natalie, because it had been carefully folded into the shape of a heart, and Francine's name was written across the front in perfect bubble letters. Francine opened it.

After we're done training Samson this afternoon, want to do makeovers?

XOXO
Nat

Francine twizzled her mouth into a knot. There *was* one other person who knew about the underwear, she realized suddenly.

Natalie.

But no way Natalie would ever fink on her, not in a

million years. Even if she did think Kansas was so cute she couldn't stop twirling her hair a mile a minute every time she saw him. She'd been on Francine's side from the beginning.

Hadn't she?

Francine shook her head. This war had made her nutty. No way Natalie would ever rat her out.

She was just about to write a response to Natalie's note when she remembered the other slip of paper. She unfolded the pink square, the thin paper crinkling between her fingers. It was a phone message, written in the secretary's thin, tight handwriting.

DATE: Dec. 8
TIME: 12:11
TO: Francine Halata, Room 43H
MESSAGE: Mother called. Working late. Francine and friend to go to father's after school. Father will pick up.

Francine stared at that third sentence for a long time. *Francine and friend to go to father's after school.*

Francine's dad was staying in a *hotel*. He'd been there for the past two weeks. Natalie couldn't go *there*. It wasn't what she was used to. She wouldn't like it.

Francine crumpled the note into a pink ball and shoved it into her desk. Then she fished out her pencil and scribbled a response to Natalie's note.

> Sorry, my mom says you can't come over today. Guess you'll have to go to your aunt's. Next week for sure. ☹
>
> Francine

She didn't even bother to try refolding it into a heart, just poked Emma in the back to ask her to pass it up. Suddenly, Francine found she didn't care all that much.

8. A CRUMPLED BALL OF PINK PAPER

When the final bell rang, Kansas couldn't have been more thrilled. It had been a miserable day, and he was looking forward to getting home as soon as possible. He was just shuffling down the aisle out of the classroom, stuffing his arms through his backpack straps, when he noticed something small and pink crumpled on the floor. It was a note from the office. And it had Francine's name on it.

Kansas stopped walking. Everyone else was streaming past him, but Kansas was fixated on that balled-up pink note on the floor. It must have fallen out of Francine's desk. Kansas knew he shouldn't look at it. He knew it was none of his business.

Kansas picked up the note.

When he was absolutely positive no one was looking, Kansas unfolded it quickly and read.

Mother called. Working late.
Francine and friend to go to father's after school.
Father will pick up.

Kansas sucked in his breath as he reread the third sentence. *Francine and friend to go to father's after school.*

"Kansas?"

Kansas's head shot up. "You forget something?" Miss Sparks asked.

"Uh . . ." Kansas looked down at the note once more, then quickly crumpled it back into a ball. "No. No, I'm fine."

"Good. I'll see you in Media Club tomorrow. Don't forget to wear your school colors. Green and white."

"Yeah," Kansas said, crossing to the front of the room. He tossed the pink note in the garbage. "School colors. Right." And he left the classroom, squeezed his way through the sea of students in the hallway, and walked across the sidewalk to the bus pick-up zone, where Ginny was waiting for him. He couldn't help thinking, the whole bus ride home, how Francine's parents were divorced. Divorced, just like his.

Somehow, that one little fact changed everything.

"No, you should put it by the dog poster. *Kan*-sas, I *said*, it looks better over there."

Kansas lowered the picture he'd been trying to put on his wall, the one of the underwear on the flagpole. He'd printed it as soon as he got home, fuzzy as it was. "*Gin*-ny," he said, in his best little-sister voice. He accidentally pressed his hand against the Scotch tape on the back of the photo, and the tape came off on his hand and got stuck between his fingers. "I told you, this is my side of the room. You have to stay on your side. Now leave me alone."

As if it weren't bad enough that Kansas's family had moved to stupid California, now Kansas had to share a room with Ginny. She always wanted to talk to him, or play with him, or bug him about one thing or another. That's why Kansas had made a barrier out of unpacked moving boxes—GINNY'S SHOES, GINNY'S SUMMER CLOTHES, all stuff his sister didn't need yet—stacked up three boxes high in the middle of the room. But last week Ginny had discovered that she could poke holes in the sides of the boxes to get things out, and now monster-sized craters appeared daily. Kansas told her if she kept it up, she was going to make the wall fall over, but she didn't seem to be listening.

"You want to see my headstand?" Ginny asked him.

"No," Kansas replied. He ripped another piece of tape off the roll and circled it over on itself, sticking it to the back to the photo. He wondered if Francine had to deal with stuff like this, sharing a room with an annoying little sister.

"I'm getting really good at headstands," Ginny said, and from the corner of his eye Kansas could see her toppling over as she attempted one. He concentrated on his Wall of Dares. "Well, Mrs. Muñoz is gonna teach me. She said she'd take me to Mommy and Me Yoga this weekend."

"Mrs. Muñoz is not your mom," Kansas told her, placing the photo just above the one of him and Ricky climbing on Will's roof. "And no way can she do a headstand. She's, like, a million."

"She's not a million. I think she's sixty. And she can too do a headstand. I saw her. She's really good at yoga, and I'm gonna do it too. She said it'd be good for my asthma."

Mrs. Muñoz was their new next-door neighbor, and she'd been watching them the past week or so, while their mom looked for a regular babysitter. She seemed nice enough, if you liked old ladies.

"I'm gonna get really good," Ginny went on, trying for another headstand. She braced her arms against the floor and kicked her feet into the air. "And then I'm gonna do headstands in the talent show. You think I could win, if I did headstands really good? It's in two weeks, and there's a prize."

"No way anyone would ever give you a prize for doing headst—"

There was a tremendous clatter as Ginny fell over on Kansas's bin of Legos, spewing them across the floor. She missed the cardboard box wall by three inches.

Kansas sighed and climbed down from his bed, picking

his way across the Lego minefield. He didn't know how much longer he could put up with all this.

"*Kan*-sas!" Ginny called as he left the room, scooping up his backpack on the way. "Where are you going? Don't you want to see me try again?"

Kansas didn't even bother to answer that one.

"Whatcha working on?"

Kansas looked up from his sheet of poster board. His mom was standing in the doorway to the kitchen, holding a thick book and a pad of notebook paper. Kansas was starting to notice that as soon as his mother got home from the gift shop, she usually grabbed one of her textbooks right away. She didn't go outside, or take a nap, or eat a snack, or any of the things she used to do when she got home from work. Now she just studied for her night class.

"Geography homework. We have to draw the whole U.S. and label the states. It's due on Monday."

"And you're working on it now?" Kansas's mother raised an eyebrow. "Is it midnight on Sunday already?"

"Ha, ha. You should be a stand-up comedian." The

truth was that doing his homework was the only way to get Ginny to stop bothering him. Ginny was as allergic to homework as she was to peanuts. As soon as she'd realized that Kansas was going to work on his map instead of watching her do headstands, she'd gone next door to bother Mrs. Muñoz.

His mother ruffled his hair. "You get a hold of Will and Ricky?" she asked.

"Nah," Kansas said, pushing his hair back in place. "They weren't at home when I called, and they're not online, either." Kansas had left the computer in the living room on, just in case, and he was still logged in to his IM account, so he'd be able to hear if they messaged him. But he didn't have his hopes up. Because even if he did manage to talk to them, what was he going to do, beg them to dump Mark H. and take him camping instead?

"Well, I'm sure they'll call back soon," his mom replied. "They're your best friends."

"Yeah," Kansas said. But he wasn't so sure anymore.

"Mind if I join you? I have homework too."

Kansas nodded, concentrating on getting the bottom tip

of Florida just right, and his mom sat next to him. Her textbook was so big, it made the whole table shake when she set it down. Kansas didn't know how anyone could read a book that big. He was never going to be a nurse. He was going to be something that didn't require any reading, like a video game tester.

While Kansas drew, copying the picture from their geography book as carefully as he could, his mother read her textbook and scribbled furious notes to herself. Every once in a while, she'd close her eyes and mumble under her breath, the way Kansas did when he was trying to memorize something.

"Test tomorrow?" he asked her.

"Big one." She flipped to a new page in her notebook, but didn't write anything. She stayed like that for a moment, pen in hand, and then she looked over at Kansas. "Feel like a grilled cheese?" she asked him.

He set down his pencil. "Sure."

"Great. Brain food. I'll get the bread, you get out the cheese."

Five minutes later, Kansas and his mom were back at the

table with their grilled cheeses and glasses of ginger ale. Kansas's mom put her feet up on the chair next to her and studied Kansas's map. "Looking pretty good," she told him.

"It looks like a headless dog," he replied, wiping a string of cheese off his chin.

She squinted at the map. "Yeah." She laughed. "A little bit. But now that I think about it, the United States is kind of doggy."

Kansas laughed back. "What's yours?" he asked.

"My homework? Anatomy. Bones of the body tonight."

"That doesn't sound so bad." Kansas took another bite of his sandwich. A whole test just for that? "How many are there?"

"Two hundred and six."

Kansas's mouth dropped open. "No way."

"Way." His mom set her sandwich down and took Kansas's left arm. "This," she said, pointing to the upper section of his arm, "is your *humerus*. And you have two bones right here." She poked him below the elbow. "The *radius*." She ran her finger along it. "And the *ulna*."

"Really?" Kansas said, taking his arm back and studying

it. He hadn't had any idea he had two bones in that part of his arm.

"Really. And there are twenty-seven in each of your hands. The *carpals,* the *metacarpals,* and the *phalanges.*"

"That sounds made-up," Kansas said. "Like animals from Australia or something."

"Now you see why I have to study so much."

"Yeah." Kansas took another bite of his sandwich and looked at his mother's textbook, open on the table. There were so many words. So many billions of things she had to memorize before she could be done with school and finally be a nurse. He looked up at her. "Can I help?" he asked.

She thought about that for a second, then took the last bite of her grilled cheese and got up from her chair. She crossed the kitchen to the junk drawer and pulled out a pack of yellow Post-its. While Kansas sat, she scribbled something with her pen on the top Post-it, then peeled it off slowly and stuck it to his shoulder.

Kansas twisted his neck to look at it.

Clavicle, the Post-it read.

"What's that?" he asked, still looking at the Post-it.

"That," his mother said, "is the name for your shoulder bone."

"Oh."

She grinned at him. "Want to see if I can get all of them in five minutes?"

Four minutes and twelve seconds later, Kansas was stuck with yellow from head to toe and his mother had almost run out of Post-its. They'd set the timer on the microwave so they'd know exactly how much time she had left to go.

"*Lumbar vertebrae!*" she shouted out, scribbling it down. "The lower back! Kansas, spin around, let me stick this on your spine." Kansas spun and his mother stuck. "Um . . ." He could practically hear the wheels turning in her brain. "*Cranium!*" She slapped a sticky on his forehead. Kansas laughed as she started to scribble a new one. "Twenty-seven seconds!" she cried, looking at the clock. "What am I missing?"

Kansas pointed to his jaw. "Is this one?" he asked.

"*Mandible!* Yes! Thanks." She scribbled, then stuck. "And *tibia*, and *fibula*." Scribble, stick, scribble, stick. "*Sacrum!*" she shouted, scribbling again.

She had just made Kansas kick off his shoes so she could slap Post-its on his toes, and the clock was down to thirteen seconds, when there was a loud *bloop!* from the living room. Kansas's head shot up. His instant messenger!

"Kansas!" his mom called as he raced for the computer, strewing Post-its across the floor. "Where are you going? We haven't finished yet!"

But Kansas was already at the computer, shaking the mouse to jump-start the screen awake.

Sure enough, there was a message in his IM window. But it wasn't from Ricky or Will.

FRANCINEHALLATA: is this kansas frm school?

Kansas stared at the screen. Francine? Francine was messaging him? Why would she do that?

"Kansas?" From the kitchen, the timer on the microwave went off. *Beep beep beep beep beeeeeeeeeeeeep!*

Slowly, Kansas stretched his Post-it-covered hands across the keyboard.

He began to type.

9.

A trained guinea pig

"Hey, pea pod," Francine's father greeted her as he pulled into the parent pick-up driveway after school. "Where's your other half?"

"Natalie wasn't at school today," Francine lied, opening the passenger's side door and dumping her backpack inside.

"I hope she's not sick again," her father replied. "That would be terrible."

"Yeah. Terrible."

"Well, I have something that will cheer you up. I brought a little surprise for you."

Francine climbed inside the car, clicked her seat belt closed, and then allowed herself to look to where her father was pointing, the backseat. This day had been miserable, start to finish, and she knew there couldn't possibly be anything back there that would cheer her up.

But she was wrong.

"Samson!" she cried.

Sure enough, there was her guinea pig, his two round eyes peeking out at her from under thick tufts of fur. He pushed himself up against the side of his cage and made the *snuffle-snuffle-gurgle-snuffle* noise that meant he wanted to be petted.

"I picked him up from the house when I went to get your clothes for tomorrow," Francine's dad told her. "I figured it was high time I saw all the little fellow's new tricks."

Francine tugged against her seat belt to wrap her dad in a tight hug around the neck. She squeezed him close, getting a good whiff of that smell she only just now realized she'd missed so deeply. In the past two weeks, Francine hadn't spent more than two days with her dad. Evening phone calls and weekend movies just weren't enough. Suddenly she was glad her mom had to work late, even if it did mean that Natalie couldn't come over.

"Thanks, Dad," she whispered.

He hugged her back. "I missed you, pea pod," he said.

Francine stayed in the hug until the smell of her father's shirt was completely familiar again. Then she whipped her door shut and shifted around in her seat to get a good look at Samson. "Hello, Sams," she greeted him, reaching back to set a hand on the top of his cage.

Snuffle-snuffle-grunt-grunt-snuffle.

The hotel her father had been staying at wasn't too far away from the school, just across the street from the Stater Bros. Market. It was different from any of the hotels Francine had ever stayed in before with her parents. This room was divided into two big areas—a bedroom of sorts, and a living room, with a fold-out couch in front of the TV for Francine to sleep on. Against the wall of the living room area there was what her father called a "kitchenette," a tiny space set up for cooking, with a stove and an oven and a sink and a mini fridge. It wasn't bad for a hotel room, Francine thought, but it wouldn't be spectacular enough to make her want to up and leave home forever.

"Okay, so here's his newest one," Francine called to her father, after she'd set up Samson's obstacle course. She was kneeling on the floor snuggling Samson, just in front of a tunnel she'd made out of her father's art books. "He's supposed to go inside the tunnel, then turn around and come back through the other way. You ready to time us?" Samson's pink nose was twitching, anxious to begin the race and snag the guinea pig treats Francine had left for him at the end.

Francine's dad snapped shut his sketchbook and stuck his pencil behind his ear. Then he squatted on the ground next to Francine and tapped a few buttons on his watch. "On your mark!" he said to Francine. She tensed her hands more tightly around Samson's back end, lifting his feet just a few inches off the ground. Samson's nose darted this way, that way, ready to race. "Get set!" Francine lowered Samson to the ground. "Go!" And she let him loose.

As soon as Samson's feet hit the floor, he was *off*.

Unfortunately, he went in completely the wrong direction, racing his way straight up Francine's T-shirt.

"Samson!" Francine cried, unhooking his claws from her shirtfront. "He did it yesterday," she told her dad. "Okay, time us again."

The second time, Samson went all the way around the tunnel and snarfed up all his treats before he'd even done anything. The third time, he sat in the middle of the tunnel and pooped.

"Well, good thing he's cute, huh?" Francine's father said as he cleaned the floor with a wad of toilet paper.

Francine had to admit that was true at least. Samson was pretty much the cutest guinea pig that ever existed, with his tufts of long silky hair that spiked out all over and his tiny pink nose. His face and his middle were white, and his butt and the top of his head were black, with one stripe of chocolate brown that stretched across his two round eyes. But if he was ever going to be a world-famous guinea pig on Francine's animal training TV show, he was seriously going to have to get his act together.

While Francine fed Samson a few more guinea pig treats, her father sat down at the table again and turned back to his sketchbook, immediately lost in thought. Francine's father was lost in thought a lot. He taught art classes at the local community college, and Francine's mother often said that his brain was like a collage, lots of pieces that didn't quite fit together but somehow managed to make art anyway. Well, her mom *used* to say that. Francine wasn't so sure her mom would think her dad's brain was art anymore.

"What are you working on?" Francine asked as Samson snuggled himself into the crook of her elbow, grunting. "A new machine?"

"Hmm?" Her dad flicked his pencil across the page a few times before looking up at her. "Oh, yes," he said, as though he'd only just heard her. "A brand-new one. Want to see?"

Francine climbed eagerly into the chair beside her father and peered down at the sketchbook in front of him.

Mostly, her dad drew portraits and cityscapes, sketched with his tiny, precise crosshatch strokes. But lately he'd taken to drawing curious sorts of inventions—chain reactions of objects and events that all led to one simple, final task. He'd told Francine once that they were called "Rube Goldberg" machines, after some famous dead guy, but Francine liked to think of them as her father's own creations. In his latest, a bowling ball was poised at the top of a large ramp, and if it were pushed, it would crash *down-down-down* into a stack of books, which would topple over to squeeze against a bottle of dish soap, which would pour out into a hanging bucket. When the bucket got heavy with soap, it would fall on top of one end of a seesaw, which would flop a teddy bear into the air, sending it careening into a basket of Ping-Pong balls . . . There were dozens of steps, and Francine pored over every one of them, until she got to the very last, where a toy car knocked over a broomstick that pushed down the lever on a toaster. Francine grinned as she counted—twenty-seven steps just to make a piece of toast.

"You think we could make one of these for real someday?" she asked her dad.

He gazed for a moment at the page in front of him. "Maybe. It would be fun, wouldn't it?"

"Totally."

He shut the sketchbook and ran his hand over the cover. "So this isn't so bad, right?" he said. "Just the two of us? Well"—he nodded at Samson—"two and a half? It's kind of cozy."

Francine shifted in her chair. It was sort of nice to have

her dad to herself for a change. "I guess," she replied. "But . . ." What he *needed* to do was come back home as soon as possible. "I don't think you should stay here forever, though."

"I'm glad you think that too," her dad said.

"You are?"

He nodded. "I've found an apartment. I move in on Sunday. I think you'll really like it."

Francine pulled another guinea pig treat out of her pocket and fed it to Samson. When he finished that one, she gave him another, before he could even squeak about it. "I think he's gotten a little bigger the past few weeks, don't you?" Francine said, examining Samson's belly. "Maybe he needs to go on a diet."

"Francine?" her father said softly. "Pea pod? You know that none of this is about you, right? Your mother and I still love you. We always will. We'll never stop being your parents, no matter what."

Francine just shrugged. Of course her parents loved her. That was their *job*. It was the way they were doing their job that bothered her. Francine might only be nine years old, but she already knew that if things weren't working out the way you planned, then you fixed them. If you weren't getting the grade you wanted in school, then you asked the teacher for extra credit. If your guinea pig wasn't doing well in his obstacle course, then you increased his training. Her parents just weren't trying hard enough. Because, sure, they argued sometimes, but no more than most people's parents. She'd seen Natalie's parents argue. Emma's, too. Alicia's parents practically murdered each other every time they drove the girls to soccer practice. But none of *them* were getting a divorce, now, were they? If only Francine knew the right thing to say, the exact right thing to do, she could fix everything. But she couldn't think of the exact right thing.

"Can we have pizza for dinner?" That's what she thought of.

Her father blinked at her for a moment, then stood and kissed Francine on the forehead. He crossed the room to get his cell. "Pepperoni and olives?"

Francine nodded. "With extra cheese."

Her father flipped through the takeout menus on the side table until he found the right one. When Francine's mom was in charge of dinner, they never ordered out, but

92

Francine's dad couldn't even cook pasta without ruining it. "So how was school today?" he asked, while he was on hold with the pizza place. "How are things going with that boy—what's his name, Arizona? Did you have to do a dare today? Did they vote you news anchor yet?"

Francine placed Samson carefully back in his cage. "His name's Kansas," she told her father. And then, between the pizza ordering and the delivery, she filled him in on her entire miserable day—minus some tiny details that she thought her dad might not want to hear about, like the part about the boys' bathroom and the principal's office.

"And he just did the dare like it was nothing!" she said, taking a bite out of her piping hot slice of pizza. "Can you believe that? He's never going to quit, and he doesn't even care about being news anchor, either. I can tell."

Francine's father offered Francine a napkin to wipe the pizza sauce off her chin. "That sounds pretty rough, pea pod. But maybe this Kansas kid isn't as awful as you think he is. It can't be easy, being the new kid in school."

"*Dad.* You can't be serious. He's *awful.* He thinks he's *so* cute and so good at everything."

"All I'm saying is that there's a second point of view to

93

every story." Her father walked to the sink to refill their plastic cups with water. "Maybe you should give him more of a chance. Who knows? Maybe he just wants to be fr—"

Her father was cut off when, from the center of the table, his cell phone began ringing. Together, Francine and her dad dug through the mound of papers and books and pizza plates to find it.

"Hello?" her father said, when at last he'd found the phone and answered it. Francine couldn't hear the voice on the other end, but she knew just from the look on her dad's face that it was someone he hadn't expected. "Yes," he said, raising an eyebrow at her. "This is Francine's father."

Francine's eyes went wide. Who was calling about *her*? Was it Mrs. Weinmore, calling to report her visit to the office?

But it couldn't be, because her dad was smiling. Laughing, almost. "Hold on," he said into the phone. "She's right here." And he handed the phone to Francine.

"Who is it?" she asked. No one ever called her on her dad's cell.

Her dad raised his eyebrows in that all-knowing fatherly

way of his that Francine found so annoying. "It's Kansas," he told her.

Kansas?

Maybe her dad was right, Francine thought, looking at the phone in his hand. Maybe Kansas did just want to be friends. Maybe he wasn't so terrible after all.

She took the phone.

"Hello?"

10. A BASKETBALL

Kansas typed his message, stared at it for a moment, and then pushed Enter.

> **kansas_the_champ: Hey francine. yeah this is me.**

In the kitchen Kansas could hear his mother putting away the Post-its in the drawer and sitting back down at the table. Probably back to studying, without even noticing he was gone. Kansas gazed at the computer screen. Twenty seconds passed. Then thirty. Still no reply from Francine.

Kansas took a deep breath. He had to type it, he decided. It was now or never. Before he chickened out. He needed to tell Francine that he'd read her note from the office and that his parents were getting divorced too. It would be nice to finally be able to talk to someone about his parents, someone who would understand. He just hoped she wouldn't be too mad about the note.

But Kansas didn't get a chance to type a single word, because suddenly there was another loud *bloop!* and a second message popped up from Francine.

> **FRANCINEHALLATA: we all took a vote on ur next dare**

Kansas squinted as he read the words. Another message popped up. Then another.

> **FRANCINEHALLATA: i 2x dog dare u to wear ur sisters tutu to school tmrw**
> **FRANCINEHALLATA: all day**

● ● ●

What Kansas needed was to cool off. He couldn't believe there had been a second in the day when he thought he might actually tell Francine about his parents. All she cared about was the stupid Media Club and being the stupid news anchor. He'd wanted to make up a super-mean dare for her too, but he hadn't gotten a chance, because she'd logged out of her IM right away.

He was planning on riding his bike, but the first thing he saw when he got outside was his basketball, sitting cold and lonely by the corner of the house. Ginny must've been playing with it. Which was stupid, really, because there was no basketball hoop. They'd had a hoop at their old house, and their mom had insisted they take it with them, but their new house didn't have a driveway, so there was nowhere to put it up. Now the hoop remained stuffed inside one of the unpacked boxes. Which, as far as Kansas was concerned, was where it could stay forever.

Kansas stood in front of the screen door for a long while, just staring at the basketball. Then, almost reluctantly, he picked it up. It did feel pretty good. He tossed it up in the air and caught it, one-handed. Then he tossed it against the side of the house, at a spot just above his and Ginny's window, and grabbed it as it bounced back his way.

As Kansas threw the ball—bounce and catch, bounce

and catch—his thoughts began to focus on the dare war. Kansas needed to think of something truly awful for Francine to do, something even worse than wearing your little sister's tutu.

But what?

Kansas aimed at the spot on the wall again—there was a scuff mark there now, exactly basketball-sized, and the dirt underneath his bedroom window was packed enough that he could almost pretend like he was dribbling. Kansas used to love playing basketball. Back in Oregon, he had even been on his school's basketball team. He'd been good too. Really good. But that was when his dad had been around to help him practice, to show up at games, to cheer for him. Kansas didn't really feel like playing much anymore.

He bent down low and dribbled five times. Then he grabbed the ball in both hands, straightened up, and shot.

The basketball hit the siding at a bad angle and flew across the yard, thumping into the Muñozes' fence next door. Kansas crossed the brown patches of grass to retrieve it.

"Hello, young man!"

Poking over the top of the fence was the head of a

gray-bearded old man in a fishing cap. "Um, hey," Kansas said. He snatched up his ball.

"You must be Ginny's brother," the man said. "I'm Ernie Muñoz. I believe you know my wife, Ramona."

"Oh." Kansas nodded. He'd heard Ginny talking about Mr. Muñoz, from when she went over there, but Kansas hadn't met him before. He'd just heard the sound of buzzing and hammering from the other side of the fence. Ginny said the guy was some kind of carpenter. "Yeah. Hey." Kansas was just turning around to go back in the house when he realized maybe he was being rude. And maybe he shouldn't be. He turned around. "I'm Kansas," he said.

"Nice to meet you, Kansas."

"You too."

"I see you have a basketball there."

This was the problem with old people, Kansas thought. They always wanted to talk to you forever, and they always said really lame stuff like, "I see you have a basketball there." What else would it be? A turnip?

"Uh, yeah."

Mr. Muñoz scratched his beard. "I saw you tossing it against the house earlier. Made quite a racket."

"Oh." So that's what this was about. Kansas had probably screwed up the old guy's nap or something. "Sorry. I have a hoop from our old house but there's nowhere to put it up." He motioned to the dirt around him.

Mr. Muñoz nodded thoughtfully and scratched at his beard again. Kansas was beginning to wonder if maybe his beard itched a lot, that maybe he had beard dandruff or something, and then he started wondering if he should make Francine wear a fake beard all day. But that wasn't mean enough.

"You know," Mr. Muñoz told him, after a bit more scratching, "there's plenty of room above our garage for a hoop, if you'd care to put it there."

Kansas looked over to the Muñozes' driveway. There *was* room for a hoop there, prime real estate. But putting your basketball hoop up on someone else's house was just . . . weird. Wasn't it? "I'd have to ask the missus, of course," Mr. Muñoz went on. "But I'm sure she'd be all right with it. She's taken quite a shine to you and your sister, I think."

"Oh. Well"—Kansas shrugged—"I don't know." What he meant was *no,* but you really couldn't say that so bluntly to an old dude with an itchy beard, now, could you? "I'll have to think about it." Maybe he could dare Francine to get dandruff? No, that didn't make any sense . . .

"Of course. You let me know."

"Sure thing." Kansas pressed the ball into his side. "Well, um . . . I'm gonna go."

"Okay, Kansas, I'll see you soon."

Kansas was just creaking open the front door when he saw it. A patch of grass, peeking out between the cracks of their front step. It looked so strange there, so odd—that patch of green where it didn't quite belong—that Kansas knew he'd come up with the perfect dare at last.

Kansas raced back into the kitchen and dug his mother's folder of school stuff out of the junk drawer. He flipped open the cover, then found the right page and scrolled his finger down until he landed on it.

Halata, Francine.

His fingers felt like they were on fire as he punched her parent contact number into the phone. This was going to be perfect, he thought. *Perfect.* The club hadn't voted on it yet, but they'd vote tomorrow morning, and it was such a good dare that Kansas was sure everyone would agree to it. Never in a million years would she do it, and then she'd be two points behind and lose the war and her precious news anchor job too. Which was exactly what she deserved.

Francine's father answered, and Kansas put on his best calm, normal voice. But when Francine picked up, he screwed his face into a sneer, prepared to really wallop her.

"Hello?" she said.

"I double dog dare you," he replied, with as much growl in his voice as he could muster up, "to dye your hair green for school tomorrow." And with that, he slammed the phone down.

11.

A bottle of green hair dye

Luckily, the store was open late. And luckily, they sold green hair dye.

Well, Francine wasn't entirely sure if it was lucky or not. When they were back at the hotel, Francine sitting sideways on the bathroom toilet and her father hovering above her with plastic gloves on and the bottle of green dye in his hands, she began to have second thoughts.

"How long does it take before it comes out again?" she asked. She'd washed and patted her hair dry already, like the instructions on the box said. The damp towel around her shoulders felt like it weighed a hundred pounds.

Her father grabbed the package off the sink and read the back. "Ten washes."

Francine thought about that. If she went through with it, it would be at least a week—probably two—before her hair was back to its normal color. Two weeks of looking like a human palm tree, every single day at school.

Her father studied her reflection in the mirror. "You sure you really want the news anchor job this badly, pea pod?"

That was one thing Francine didn't need to think about. TV animal-trainers-to-be were meant to be in front of cameras, not behind them. She nodded, one sharp jerk of her head. Then she took a deep breath. "Do it," she told her father.

"Okay . . . ," he said. And Francine watched in the mirror as he tilted the bottle over her head, squeezed, and . . .

Splat!

Francine Halata could no longer call herself a blonde.

12. A SPARKLY WHITE TUTU

Kansas had had a lot of nightmares in his life. Nightmares about skeletons chasing him, and having to jump off mile-high cliffs into pits of bubbling lava, and vampires with machine guns for fangs. But wearing his little sister's sparkly white tutu on his second Friday at his new school turned out to be worse than anything Kansas could have dreamed up in a thousand years. Even for the King of Dares, this one was a doozy.

Kansas walked up the front steps, eyes straight ahead, tugging tight on his backpack straps. He took each step casually and quickly, in a way that said, "Yes, I know I'm wearing a tutu, thank you. I think it looks pretty awesome."

At least he hoped it said that. But he was pretty sure it didn't. How could he look awesome in a *tutu*? He'd worn a plain white T-shirt that morning, thinking that it would blend in and make the tutu less noticeable, but the second Kansas had caught his reflection in the bus window that morning, he'd realized that it didn't make him less noticeable. It made him look like a swan.

Beside him, Ginny took his hand and squeezed it. "Don't worry, Kansas," she told him. "I think you look good. Just like a real ballerina."

After Kansas dropped Ginny off at Art Club, he focused his eyes on his feet. The waistband of the tutu was too tight, and it itched, too, chafing his belly with every step. And was it just him, or had the hallway gotten longer since yesterday? And more full of kids? Kansas's senses were suddenly on hyperalert. He could hear every snicker of the swim team over by the lockers, laughing at him. He could feel the air rustling from every mathlete who whipped a head in his direction. And the fingers of all the yearbook members pointing at him were practically in Technicolor. One of the Basketball Club kids over by the

K.B.

gym shouted, "Hey! Nice dress!" And the whole hallway broke out in screams of laughter.

Five feet from Miss Sparks's door, Kansas felt a tap on his shoulder. He whirled around.

Francine.

"Nice tutu," she told him.

"Nice hair," he replied. Her smirk quickly faded into a frown.

Kansas almost couldn't believe she'd really done it. But she had. Francine's new green hair hung down in front of her face like vines in a jungle.

"I can't believe you made me do this," she said, jabbing a finger toward her head. "You're so mean. I would never do anything that mean to you."

"*I'm* so mean?" Kansas replied.

The door whipped open.

"Why, hello there, you two!" It was Miss Sparks, white teeth flashing. "I thought I heard some students out here. Come inside, won't you? You both look incredible, by the way."

Incredible? Kansas was pretty sure that what they looked like was two circus freaks.

Kansas was heading to his desk with his head down, pretending to ignore the whispers of his fellow club members, when Miss Sparks clapped her hands together. Suddenly, every head in the class was turned his way.

"Good morning, Media Club!" she said. "Before we get started on today's announcements, I want you all to take a good look at Kansas and Francine."

Kansas's insides turned to Jell-O. What was going on? Had Miss Sparks finally had it with the dares? Was she going to make an *example* of them? Next to him, Francine looked equally perplexed.

From the back of the room, Luis snapped a picture.

"Everyone," Miss Sparks went on. She put one hand on Kansas's shoulder and the other on Francine's. "This"— Kansas closed his eyes and waited for the humiliation to go away—"*this* is what true school spirit looks like."

"Huh?" Kansas's eyes popped open.

"What?" Francine said.

"Today," Miss Sparks continued, "is School Spirit Day. We were all told to wear our school colors, green and white. And I see a few of you who tried"—she nodded at Alicia, in the far corner, wearing a green dress, and Natalie, with a flowery green and white headband—"but no one put as much effort into their school spirit today as Kansas and Francine here, and I think that's really commendable, don't you?"

Commendable? Kansas looked down at his white tutu, and then up at Francine's grass-green hair. Well, how about that? Maybe they *were* commendable.

Miss Sparks squeezed his shoulder. "As you all know, Mrs. Weinmore will be visiting every classroom this morning to see which class has the most school spirit, and the winning class gets an ice cream party this afternoon. And I'd be willing to bet that with Kansas and Francine on our side, we just may be the ones to win it."

There was a cheer from somewhere in the back of the room, and then a squeal of *"Ice cream!"* And before Kansas knew what had happened, there was applause and a chant of "Kansas and Francine! Kansas and Francine!" And slowly, bit by bit, Kansas began to feel less like a dork in a tutu, and more like a champion of the fourth grade.

"Francine and Kansas," Miss Sparks went on, her teeth flashing full force, "I really have to hand it to you two. Not only did you wear the school colors, but you did it in a way that demonstrates your commitment to teamwork, which is what school spirit at Auden Elementary is really all about. It truly is an extraordinary effort on both your parts. I think this just goes to show that with the two of you working together, amazing things can happen."

Kansas glanced sideways at Francine. He could tell, from the look of burning hatred in her eyes, that for once in her life, she was thinking the exact same thing that he was.

There was no way that the two of them would ever, *ever,* work together.

13.

A towering stack of CDs

When Francine's mother opened the curtains on Sunday morning to let the light stream across Francine's bed, Francine was less than super thrilled about it.

"Mmmm-fwuhp-aggh!" she cried, thrusting the crook of her elbow across her eyes to block the sun.

"Good morning to you too, darling," her mother said. And Francine could tell, without even looking at her, that her mother had a smile on her face.

"I thought it was Sunday," Francine said from underneath her arm.

"It is Sunday, sleepyhead." Her mother sat on the edge of Francine's bed and gently removed Francine's arm from her face. "We're going to morning yoga today. Won't that be fun?"

Francine frowned. "Can't we go to morning yoga after lunch?" she said, and she rolled over onto her side, planted her face in her vine-green hair, and pulled her blankets over her head.

"Oh, now, silly, come on," her mom said, tossing back all of Francine's blankets. Francine's chilly toes immediately curled up in protest. "We've been planning on going to Mommy and Me Yoga for ages, and we never get around to it. But today's the day. Up, now. That's a girl." And she hoisted Francine up by the armpits.

"*Mmmmfle-blug,*" Francine replied.

That proved to not be enough of a compelling argument for Francine's mother. By eight forty-five, they were sitting at the breakfast table, Francine's hands wrapped around a salmon-asparagus wrap.

"Breakfast," her mother told her, as though maybe if she hadn't clarified, Francine would have thought it was a snow boot. Francine took a bite before she was awake enough to remember that she hated salmon-asparagus wraps.

The phone rang, and her mother picked it up. "It's Natalie," she said, handing the cordless to Francine.

Francine swallowed her bite. "Hey," she said into the phone. "What's up?"

"Can I come over now to help train Samson?" Natalie asked. She sounded like she'd already eaten breakfast, brushed her teeth, and done forty jumping jacks. "My dad said he'd drive me over when you woke up, and now you're awake, so I'm coming. You want to work on climbing up ramps today?"

"My mom's making me do *yoga*." Francine rubbed the sleep out of her eyes. "But definitely after I get back. I have lots of good ideas."

"Cool," Natalie said. "Call me as soon as you get home. And when we're done with training, I can do your hair."

"My hair?"

"Yeah. I'm gonna give you a makeover. I have some ideas to make you look less slimy."

"Okay," Francine said with a laugh. "Well, I'll see you then."

"Bye!"

Francine hung up the phone and went back to her breakfast wrap. Talk about slimy, she thought, taking a bite.

As Francine chewed, her mother sat across from her, staring, one hand wrapped around her tea mug. It took Francine a moment to realize that what her mother was staring at was *her.*

"Mom?" she said. "You okay?"

Her mother blinked. "Oh. No, I'm fine. I . . ."

"Mom?"

"It's just . . ." She heaved a deep sigh. "It wasn't some sort of preteenage rebellion thing, was it?"

"Huh?" Sometimes talking to parents was like trying to crack a code.

"Your *hair,*" her mother replied. She lifted her mug to her mouth, but then set it down again without taking a sip. "I mean, I know you said you did it because that boy dared you, but I can't help wondering if this is your way of . . . What I mean is . . . are you upset about the divorce?"

Francine rolled her eyes. Jeez, her parents went and got one idiotic divorce and suddenly that was the only thing either of them could talk about. "I told you, I did it so I could be the news anchor at school." She took an enormous bite of her breakfast wrap. Even eating salmon and asparagus was better than having this conversation. "Not everything I do is because of you and Dad, you know."

Her mother stared into her mug for a long minute, silent. Then she got up, walked to the sink, and poured all her tea slowly down the drain. When she turned around, she leaned against the sink, arms jutting out from her sides, and studied Francine. "I think it looks nice," she said at last. "Your hair. It's unusual. And sort of lovely."

Francine squinted one eye at her mother. If Francine had gone and dyed her hair green a month ago, her mom would *not* have said it was lovely. She would've grounded her until she was old enough to vote. Maybe getting a divorce made you nutty. "I look like a frog," she told her mother. She wadded her napkin into a ball. "And it's never gonna come out, either." Francine had already shampooed her hair thirteen times in the past two days, and it was still as green as a fern. And the worst part was that she couldn't even come up with any terrible dares to get Kansas back.

After Friday morning, the Media Club had decided that Francine and Kansas couldn't dare each other anymore. Even if the two of them *had* accidentally won the class an ice cream party, the other members were slightly miffed that they hadn't gotten to vote on their dares ahead of time. So now every dare had to come from them. It made sense, really, Francine thought. But a lot of good it did her now. She was still losing—three points to four—and at this rate it looked like she might never catch up.

"I'm going to be a frog forever," she said.

Her mother considered that for a moment. Then she pushed herself away from the counter. "I have an idea," she said, grabbing Francine's hand and hoisting her to her feet.

After leading Francine to the armchair in the front room, her mother plopped her down and told her to wait. "I need supplies!" she said, disappearing down the hallway. When she returned, she had a fistful of bobby pins and hair ties. Francine craned her neck around to inspect them, but her mother twisted her head forward again. "It's a surprise," she said. And she proceeded to brush and yank and tug at Francine's hair, not in a way that hurt, but carefully, gently, the way she used to when Francine had been really little.

"Don't we have to go to yoga?" Francine asked.

"We have a few minutes. Keep your head up. There."

Francine's mother twisted and tucked, parted and pleated, until finally she announced, "All done!" She stuck the last bobby pin deep into Francine's hair. "Come on, I'll show you in the mirror."

Francine followed her mother to the bathroom, where she was turned around in front of the mirror. Her mom raised a handheld mirror in front of her face so Francine could see the back of her hair.

It was all braids. Big ones and small ones, curled over and around one another. One large, green maze of hair.

"I love it," Francine said, gazing at herself. "Thank you."

"See?" Her mom set her head on top of Francine's so that their faces were one on top of the other in the mirror. "You're not a frog at all. You're a frog princess."

Besides the teacher, there were only nine people at Mommy and Me Yoga. Which made sense, Francine thought, because who wanted to go to yoga while you were still digesting breakfast? There was a skinny twelve-year-old boy who wore his sweat shorts up so high they were practically under his armpits. Both he and his mother looked much too serious for yoga. The curly-haired sisters and their mother were all so stretchy that Francine could tell they'd been going to yoga for ages. There was also an older lady with a girl who was probably about five or six, the youngest of the group. The girl had her brown hair pulled into a sloppy ponytail, and she spent most of the time falling over and giggling. Francine thought that maybe the older lady was the girl's grandmother, until she heard the girl call her Mrs. Muñoz.

Francine tried her best to stand straight as a board with her left foot in the crook of her right knee, but no matter how many times the instructor, Lulu, told her to "focus your mind to find your balance," Francine kept falling over. She decided Lulu was the one who was unbalanced.

"Isn't this great?" Francine's mother asked while they were doing downward-facing dog, their butts up in the air and their legs stretched almost to breaking behind them. "I can feel all my stress just melting away. We're definitely coming next week."

Francine didn't even have the energy to argue.

After the class was over, Francine's mother went to the front desk to sign them up for a month of lessons and Francine plopped herself on the bench outside the classroom to wait. She hadn't been sitting there three seconds when the giggly girl with the sloppy ponytail sat down beside her.

"Hi," the girl said. "I'm Ginny."

Francine just shrugged. She wasn't in the mood for chatting.

But apparently Ginny was. "What's your name?" she asked.

"Francine."

"I like your hair." Ginny kicked her feet in the air.

"Anyone want a snack?"

Francine looked up. Lulu was standing in front of them with a bowl of granola bars. "I always like to keep a few for my students. Just in case they need a little sustenance after class."

Francine shrugged again and dug a granola bar out of the bowl.

"Ginny?" Lulu said, offering her the bowl.

Ginny shook her head. "I'm allergic."

Francine ripped open her granola bar as Lulu went to talk to the parents. Next to her, Ginny kept swinging her legs. Francine sort of wanted to ask her to stop, because she was shaking the whole bench, but that would involve talking, and Francine wasn't really in the mood.

"Have you ever seen *The Parent Trap*?" Ginny asked suddenly.

Francine looked up.

"My friend Stephanie at school was talking about it," Ginny went on. "I've never seen it. It sounds really good."

Francine nodded. She'd seen that movie, years ago. It was about twin girls who tricked their divorced parents into falling in love again so they'd get remarried. She took a bite of her granola bar. "Yeah," she said in between chews. "It's okay."

"Mrs. Muñoz said she'd rent it for me. I wanna watch it 'cause my parents are getting divorced."

Francine stopped chewing. "Oh," she said.

"Stephanie said in the movie they make their parents have, like, a really romantic date, and then they remember how much they love each other. You think something like that would work on my parents?"

Francine plucked a granola crumb from where it had landed on her T-shirt. "Maybe," she said, popping the crumb in her mouth.

"I bet my brother'd help me," Ginny said, back to swinging her feet again. "He's real nice. He loves helping me. Except when he's doing his homework. He has homework a lot. He's real smart. What would you do if your parents were getting divorced?"

Francine licked the stickiness off her fingers. "How can you be allergic to granola bars?" she asked. "I've never heard of that."

Luckily, Ginny didn't seem to notice that Francine had changed the subject. "It's not really granola bars," she explained, swinging her legs even higher. "It's peanuts. If I eat a single bite of a peanut, my face'll blow up red and hivey, and I have to go to the hospital right away or I could keel over."

"But then you should just get one that's not peanut flavor," Francine replied. "See?" She held out her granola bar wrapper for Ginny to examine. "Chocolate chip."

Ginny shook her head. "There's peanut traces. Everything has 'em, almost. Granola bars, bread, chocolate, chili sometimes." She counted them off on her fingers. "I gotta check everything. Mom says I'm a pain in the neck to shop for." She grinned.

"You can't eat *chocolate*?" Francine had never heard of anything so terrible.

"Check the wrapper if you don't believe me. I'll bet you a headstand."

Francine flattened the wrapper to read the ingredients. Sure enough, Ginny was right. It was right there on the label: "This product may contain peanut traces."

"Headstand!" Ginny cried.

Even after a full hour of yoga, Francine couldn't do a headstand to save her life. She tried it with her eyes closed. She tried it holding her breath. She tried it with her back braced against the wall. Each time, she fell—*plop!*—on the floor in a heap. After the fifth try, Ginny joined her, but she turned out to be no better than Francine. Soon they were both giggling, tumbling out of one headstand, then another. They decided to make up their own yoga poses instead, and Ginny told Francine more about her older brother, who sounded smart and funny and brave.

"He's super good at basketball too," Ginny told her as she twisted her arms around her torso like a human tornado. "He's practically in the NBC."

"You mean the NBA?" Francine asked. She was halfway bent against the wall, one hand next to her head, and the other stretched out for balance.

"Yeah, that one."

"I see you've finally taken to yoga," Francine's mother said, coming back over to retrieve her.

Francine looked at her mother's upside-down face. "I call this one 'downward-facing guinea pig,'" she said, just before Ginny sneak-attack tickled her in the armpit and she fell over laughing once more.

"You're coming next week, right, Franny?" Ginny asked.

Normally Francine hated it when people called her Franny, but Ginny was so cute, she somehow didn't mind so much. "Yep," she told her. "You too?"

"You bet."

Francine's mother smiled as they walked to the car. "See, now, that wasn't so terrible, was it?"

Francine grunted in reply. Sometimes, she had discovered, it was best not to let parents know when they were right.

It wasn't until they were half a block from home that Francine spotted the familiar blue sedan parked in their driveway. "Dad's here!" she shouted.

Her mother did not respond. Instead, she inched the car toward their house and stopped in front of their driveway. She didn't pull in, even though there was plenty of room next to Francine's father's car. She just stopped the car, right there in the middle of the street, and stared at the empty spot in the driveway.

"Mom?" Francine said. "Why aren't you parking?"

Francine's mother rested her hands on the steering wheel. "What do you say we go out for frozen yogurt?" she asked.

Francine looked at the clock. "It's eleven o'clock," she said.

"The diner, then?" Her mother smoothed her hands across the steering wheel. "You could get strawberry pancakes."

The last time Francine had tried to order strawberry pancakes at the diner, her mother had told her she might as well inject sugar directly into her veins. "I want to go see Dad," she said, and she opened her door.

"Francine," her mother said, but Francine ignored her, stretching one leg out of the car. *"Francine!"*

Francine pulled her leg, slowly, back into the car and turned to look at her mother.

Her mom took a long breath, in and out.

"Your father's moving to a new apartment this afternoon," she said at last. "He's at our house so he can pack, and I told him we'd stay out of his hair while he . . . I didn't think it would take so long. I should've . . . let's go to the diner, huh? I just think it will be easier if we give your dad some time to himself."

Easier? Francine thought. Easier for who? She looked at her mom, and she looked at the house.

Francine stretched her leg back outside the car.

"Francine!" her mom called again. But Francine didn't care. She loped across the driveway and opened the front door. "Dad!" she cried into the living room. "We're back!"

She didn't get any farther than the doorway.

Boxes. There were boxes everywhere, half packed, with newspapers sticking out of them, and garbage bags stuffed with clothes. Her father was sitting on the couch, sorting through a towering stack of CDs.

"Hi, pea pod," he greeted her, rising to his feet. "I didn't think I'd see you until tomorrow."

Francine could feel a lump forming in the back of her throat, and she didn't like it. If she was smarter, this never would have happened. If she knew how to fix things, like those girls in *The Parent Trap,* this would all go away.

"Hey," she choked out.

Her mother appeared in the doorway behind her and draped an arm across Francine's body, her car keys jangling against Francine's shoulder. "Donald," she said.

Francine's father darted his eyes back to the stack of CDs. "Cecily. Nice to see you."

And then they stood there. They stood there, the three

of them, in their own house, with the door open, for a good two minutes, not talking. Like they didn't even *know* each other.

When the phone rang, Francine raced to answer it, thankful that finally something in the house was making noise.

"Hello?"

"Hey, Francine, it's me!"

"Huh?" Francine didn't recognize the voice at first. She was too busy staring at her mother, standing stiff as a plank in the doorway, studying her keys like they were rubies.

"It's me, silly, Natalie! Can I come over now?"

Francine's father was tossing CDs into a box so fast you'd think he was going for the world record. *Clack-clack-clack-clack-clack-clack!* He'd probably broken thirty cases already.

"Francine?"

"Uh, now's not really a good time. I have, um, chores."

"I could help you," Natalie said. "I'm a good vacuumer. Ask your parents. I'm sure they'll say yes."

"I just—"

"I really want to give you a makeover. I found lots of good hairstyles on this website. You're gonna look so good, no one'll even notice your hair is green."

Francine's mother was sorting through the mail on the table by the door. She still hadn't moved five feet into the house. Francine's father had his head buried so far into the box of CDs he looked like he might suffocate.

"My mom already fixed it," Francine said. "My hair."

"She did?"

"Yeah. It looks really good. I'll show you tomorrow at school, 'kay?"

"But—"

"I gotta go. I'll call you later. Bye!"

And Francine hung up the phone.

Francine and her father spent the whole rest of the afternoon packing up his stuff, while her mother went on an impromptu shopping trip. Shirt by shirt, magazine by magazine, it all went into boxes—books, shaving cream, the diploma off his office wall, everything. In the end, it wasn't as bad as Francine had thought it would be. She and her dad had banana sandwiches and chocolate milk shakes for lunch, and Francine's father put on all his favorite CDs, and they danced their best tooshy-shaking dance moves as they taped up all his boxes. It wasn't *fun,* exactly, dividing a house in two. But it wasn't awful, either.

No, Francine realized after her mother returned late that afternoon with nothing to show for her shopping trip but one bottle of expensive-looking hand lotion, the sad part was realizing that her parents were really only her parents anymore when the other one wasn't around.

14. THREE GOLF BALLS

"Does it look level?" Mr. Muñoz called down from the ladder. He was holding the basketball hoop over his head, against the front of the garage, while Kansas steadied the ladder. Kansas was worried Mr. Muñoz was going to fall off and bite it on the pavement, but Mr. Muñoz had insisted he do it.

"It looks good!" Kansas hollered back at him.

Kansas had finally given up and let Mr. Muñoz put the hoop in his driveway. It would be nice to have somewhere to shoot, and anyway, it seemed like Mr. Muñoz really needed something to do while his wife and Ginny were at their yoga class.

"Great, thanks!" Mr. Muñoz marked where to drill the holes with a pencil, then carefully climbed back down the ladder and set the hoop on the driveway. He picked up his power drill and nodded toward the toolbox. "I need a nine-sixty-fourths," he said.

"Huh?" Kansas asked.

Mr. Muñoz looked up from where he was loosening the tip of the drill. "You know about drill bits?" he asked Kansas.

Kansas kicked his toes against the driveway. Was that something he was supposed to know? "No. Not really."

"Bring them here. I'll show you."

So Mr. Muñoz told Kansas all about drill bits—different sizes and how to know which one you needed—and showed him how to screw them into the drill and how to engage it so you could drill stuff and how to lock it so you didn't accidentally drill your eye out, that sort of thing.

"Cool," Kansas said, pressing the button on the drill to make it *whirrrrrrrr.* It vibrated in his hand. "You know all this stuff from being a carpenter?"

Mr. Muñoz scratched his beard. "That's right. Been

working with tools for a long time. You know, I'm always looking for help on projects, if you're up for it."

Kansas shrugged. Drilling and hammering and stuff sounded cool, but he knew from experience that when grown-ups said they wanted your help, they didn't really mean it. Every time his dad had asked him to help with something around the house, he'd just ended up grumbling that kids didn't know a hammer from a hole in the wall and then taking it over himself. "I'll think about it," Kansas said.

"No problem." Mr. Muñoz handed the drill back to Kansas. "You want to drill the holes?"

"Really?"

"Sure. Just make sure you hit the pencil marks. I'll hold the ladder."

Kansas started up the ladder, one careful step at a time, gripping the drill in his right hand. When he got to the top, he looked down at Mr. Muñoz.

"Go ahead!" Mr. Muñoz shouted, both hands on the ladder. "I've got you!"

Kansas found the topmost pencil mark on the left and

aligned the drill bit with it, at a right angle, just like Mr. Muñoz had showed him. Then he made sure the power button was engaged, and he started drilling.

Whirrrrrrrrr!

The drill only made a dent at first, the wood coming out in tiny spiral slivers. But then all at once the drill powered through with a jolt. Kansas put it in reverse and pulled the bit out.

"I made the first hole!" he hollered down.

"Aces!" Mr. Muñoz called up to him.

Kansas grinned to himself. *Aces,* he thought.

And he was aces for the second and third hole too. Just one more left and then they could attach the hoop with the screws, and Kansas would be able to dribble and shoot like a real basketball player again. He was almost sad he hadn't signed up for Basketball Club after all. *Almost.*

Kansas was halfway through drilling the last hole when there was a loud honk from the street behind him. Kansas ignored it. It was rickety up on that ladder, and he needed to stay focused.

Honk! Honk!

Kansas kept drilling—*whirrrrrrrrr!*—as Mr. Muñoz addressed whoever it was in the car. "Can I help you?" he called.

Whirrrrrrrrr!

"I'm looking for Grove Street!" came a voice from below. "You know where it is?"

Whirrrrrrrrr!

"Well, you're on Grove," Mr. Muñoz shouted back, still holding on to the ladder. "Which house do you want?"

Whirrrrrrrrr!

"I forgot to write down the number," the voice said. "But maybe you know the family I'm looking for? Susie Bloom? Two kids, Kansas and Ginny?"

Kansas stopped drilling and whirled around on the ladder. Could it be? No.

But it was.

Kansas dropped the drill with a terrible clatter, just missing Mr. Muñoz's head.

The man in the car was Kansas's dad.

● ● ●

"Okay, I've got a red, an orange, and a blue," Kansas's dad said.

"Orange!" Ginny squealed.

Kansas's father tossed Ginny the golf ball. "Kansas?" he asked.

Kansas rammed his golf club into the ground. "I don't care," he grumbled.

"Red it is." His father handed him the red ball, and Kansas shoved it in his jacket pocket. It was too cold to go miniature golfing. Who went mini golfing in the middle of December?

Ginny clapped her hands together as they walked toward the first hole. "I get to go first, 'cause I'm the youngest, right?" she asked.

Her father grinned and hoisted her onto his shoulder, singing at the top of his lungs, *"Come on, come on down, sweet Virginia!"* Ginny squealed and flailed her golf club around wildly as her father tickled her behind the knees. *"Come on, come on down, I beg of you!"*

Kansas rolled his eyes and ducked out of the way of Ginny's golf club. Ginny always loved when their dad sang that song to her.

"Are we gonna play or what?" he asked.

Kansas's father swung Ginny down from his shoulder and planted her feet firmly on the ground. "Yes, sir!" he said, giving Kansas a salute. Ginny giggled.

Kansas did not exactly want to be spending his Sunday afternoon at the Barstow Putt-Putt with Ginny and their father. He'd rather be anywhere else in the world, really. But no one had asked him what he wanted.

"Mom didn't even tell us you were coming, you know," Ginny said as she lined up her first shot. Kansas could already tell that there was no way her ball was going to make it up the ramp to the windmill. She was aiming too far left.

Kansas's dad stood behind Ginny and inched her golf club more in line with the shot. "She didn't know," he said, holding Ginny's arms as she took a practice swing. "I didn't know myself, actually. I was just sort of driving around last night, nowhere in particular to go, and I thought, hey, I miss the munchkins. I should go see them. And here I am." Together he and Ginny swung the club, and the ball flew— *smack!*—straight up the ramp into the windmill.

"That's a twelve-hour drive without stops," Kansas said. He knew it was twelve hours because when he and his mom and Ginny had moved he'd timed it, smooshed up in the U-Haul with all their pillows and blankets and winter coats, and Ginny singing "Coming 'Round the Mountain" in his ear until she finally passed out.

"Ten the way I drive," his father said with a grin. "Anyway, it was worth it." He ruffled Ginny's hair. "Aren't you glad I'm here?"

"Totally," Ginny said.

Kansas didn't answer.

"You're next, champ," Kansas's dad told him. "You remember how I showed you to line it up?"

"I remember," Kansas grumbled. He pulled the ball out of his pocket, lined it up, and got it through the windmill in one.

"Nice!" his dad exclaimed.

When they were all on the main part of the first hole, putting into the cup, Kansas's dad asked him, "So, how's the new school going so far, champ? You up to anything exciting?"

What Kansas *wanted* to say was that his dad would know exactly what he was up to if he bothered to call, like, ever.

But what he did say was, "No, not really." He putted his ball into the hole and marked two strokes on the scorecard.

"Nothing at all?" his dad asked as Ginny lined up her shot. "You must be doing something fun."

Ginny swung and missed, then missed again. "He's in the newspaper club at school," she told their father. "Aren't you, Kansas?"

"Newspapers?" their dad asked. "That sounds pretty boring, doesn't it?"

"It's *Media* Club," Kansas replied. "And I think it's awesome. It's the best club in the whole school, and everyone wants to be in it. I'm going to be the news anchor next semester." Well, he probably would be. After last Friday's dare, he was ahead four to three.

Ginny swung her sixth stroke and finally gave up, picking up her ball and plunking it in the hole. "I got six," she told Kansas. He marked it down.

"News anchor doesn't sound so bad," Kansas's father said as they walked to the second hole. It was the one with the swinging log in front of the hole. Kansas hated that kind. "But newspapers?" He scrunched up his face. "I thought you were going to do basketball again this year. You were always pretty good at basketball."

"This school doesn't have basketball," Kansas told him.

"Yes they do," Ginny said. "'Member? Mom kept telling you to sign up, but you picked newspapers instead."

"I didn't have anywhere to practice," Kansas replied.

"But Mr. Muñoz—"

Kansas poked her in the stomach.

"You know what we should do?" Kansas's father said suddenly. "Tomorrow I'll take you to the park. Huh, champ? I saw one near here, when I was looking for your house, and it had a great basketball court. Then you and I can get some practice in. And we can show Ginny here a couple moves too."

Ginny was already jumping up and down with excitement. You'd think going to the park was the most amazing thing that had ever happened to her in her whole life.

Their father laughed. "Well, it's settled then. I'll pick you two up after school, and we'll go to the park and shoot some hoops."

"But Mom—" Kansas started.

"I'll work it all out with your mother, don't you worry. All right, who shoots first on this hole? Kansas?"

After they'd finished all eighteen holes, their dad went inside to buy churros and soda while Kansas and Ginny waited at the tables outside. Kansas folded an old straw wrapper into an accordion, and Ginny bounced in her seat.

"Hey, Kansas, guess what," she said.

"What?" he grumbled. She was rocking the bench so hard, Kansas felt like they were about to blast off into space.

"Dad's gonna move here."

Kansas looked up. "To the Putt-Putt?"

"No, silly. To California. Right near us."

Kansas went back to his straw wrapper. "No he's not," he said.

"Yes he is. He said so."

"No," Kansas said, "he's not."

"He *told* me. When you were in the bathroom. He said the weather was really nice here and he missed us and he was gonna move here. And then we'll see him all the time and—"

"Ginny!" Kansas shouted. He couldn't take it anymore. "He's *not* gonna move here. He's gonna leave again soon, just like before. So don't get too used to having him around."

Ginny narrowed her eyes at him. "You're mean," she told Kansas. "He is too gonna move here, you'll see. You don't know what you're talking about."

Kansas let out a puff of air so strong that it blew his straw-wrapper accordion across the table. "Fine," he told Ginny. It wasn't worth the fight. He could see their father across the patio, walking toward them with their churros and sodas. He'd bought nachos and ice cream too. "I'm sorry."

"You better be," Ginny replied, just as their dad sat down beside them.

Kansas had known their dad a lot longer than Ginny—three years longer—and he knew that he wasn't going to move to California, not ever, no matter what he said. Ginny was dead wrong for thinking he would. Kansas knew she was.

But, just for a second, Kansas wished he didn't know it.

15.

Eighty-seven packets of ketchup

The bucket at the end of the lunch line in the school cafeteria held eighty-seven packets of ketchup. Francine knew that for a fact, because every last one of them was currently piled in front of her in an enormous heap.

"You gotta hurry," Alicia said from across the lunch table. "You only have till the bell rings."

Francine picked a packet off the table. "All of them?" she asked, hoping no one else could hear the quiver in her voice.

"That was the dare," Luis replied. He frowned, as though he was starting to feel bad about his vote. *I double dog dare you to eat every single ketchup packet in the bucket in the cafeteria,* that was the dare Brendan had given her that morning. And everyone in the Media Club had voted on it, unanimously. Even Natalie. It was totally unfair, Francine thought. All Kansas had to do was howl like a wolf every time someone said his name.

From the corner of the lunch table, Kansas folded his arms across his chest and grinned at her. "You ready to give up yet?" he said. "Because then you'd lose another point and it'd be five points to thr—"

Francine scowled at him. "You haven't earned your fifth point yet," she said, *"Kansas."*

Kansas scowled right back at her, then opened up his mouth and . . .

"Aaaaaaaah-OOOOOOOH!"

Howled like a wolf.

Francine allowed herself a tiny smile. Maybe the dare they'd given Kansas was a pretty good one after all. She ripped off the corner of her ketchup packet.

She held it up to her mouth.

And she squeezed.

"That's one," she said after she'd swallowed all the ketchup down. She slapped the empty packet on the table. "Give me another one."

Luis quickly ripped open another packet and handed it to Francine. "Two," he said as she gulped.

It turned out that getting the ketchup dare wasn't the worst thing to happen to Francine that day. The worst thing was that Natalie wouldn't even look at her, wouldn't even *glance* at her. Natalie hadn't spoken to Francine once since they arrived at Media Club that morning, even when Francine had tried to explain about uninviting her to her house yesterday. And at first recess, Natalie had given Alicia her pudding cup. *Alicia.* She even let her have the plastic spoon.

Francine squeezed out the twenty-first ketchup packet. The back of her neck was starting to sweat.

Twenty-two. Her eyes were starting to water.

Twenty-three. Her head was just the tiniest bit achy.

Across the table, Alicia whispered something to Natalie, and they both giggled. Francine snatched another ketchup packet off the table and ripped it open.

Forty-four. Francine could feel her second wind coming on. She was guzzling ketchup faster than ever.

Fifty-one. Emma and Luis were now cheering her on, chanting, "*Fran*-cine! *Fran*-cine!"

Sixty-two. Francine was still going strong, although she

had to take a short break when Mr. DuPree passed by their table. Luis tossed his coat over the empty ketchup packets so he wouldn't notice that they'd violated the two-ketchups-per-student rule.

Seventy. Francine burped. It smelled like rotten tomatoes. Everyone at the table inched back in their seats.

"Only two minutes till the lunch bell rings," Brendan told her. "Feel like quitting yet?" Francine shook her head and soldiered on.

Seventy-one. Francine wiped her forehead. A long strand of green hair had fallen out of its braid, and she could feel ketchup smeared on her cheeks.

Seventy-five. She was going to make it. She would. She *had* to.

Eighty-three. Francine took a packet from Luis, and her hand shook as she held it. She stared at the ketchup for a minute, breathing deep, worried breaths. She just needed a moment. Everyone around the table sat silent, waiting.

Francine ate the ketchup.

Eighty-four. The group was becoming more excited than ever. Luis and Emma were chanting loudly, and even Alicia and Andre had joined in. "*Fran*-cine! *Fran*-cine!"

Eighty-five. Just two more left to finish.

Eighty-six. Emma cheered. Luis clapped. Alicia whooped. And then . . .

Ga-LOOP!

It was a distinctly awful sound, the sound of Francine's lunch turning over in her stomach. Francine could tell by the look on the faces of everyone at the table that they had all heard it too. She felt queasier than she ever remembered feeling in her life. Eighty-six packets of ketchup, it turned out, was a lot.

"Are you gonna hurl?" Brendan asked, the sneer bright and clear on his face. "'Cause if you barf up all the ketchup, it doesn't count."

"Yeah," Andre agreed. "Barfing doesn't count."

Francine swallowed hard. "I'm not going to barf," she said. But—*ga-LOOP!*—her stomach disagreed.

From the corner of the table, Kansas frowned at her. "You don't look so good," he said. "Maybe you should go to the nurse's office."

"*You* don't look so good," Francine shot back, wiping the sweat off her forehead, *"KAN-sas."*

The wolf-howling *"Aaaaaaaah-OOOOOOOH!"* that

Kansas reluctantly unleashed was enough to get Francine through her very last packet of ketchup, number eighty-seven.

Francine dropped her head on the table. She'd done it. She had four points. At least for the moment, she and Kansas were tied.

Ga-LOOP!

Francine lifted her head, a ketchup packet pasted to her forehead. "Maybe I do need to go to the nurse's office," she said. She peeled the ketchup away from her head, slowly, then pulled one leg out from under the table and over the bench.

"I'll go with you!" Emma said, leaping up from the table. She grabbed Francine under the armpit and hoisted her to her feet. "You okay?" she asked as they walked out of the cafeteria.

Francine glanced back at the table, where Brendan was continuing to make Kansas howl like a wolf and Alicia was continuing to make Natalie giggle. "Yeah, I'll be fine," she said, draping her arm across Emma's shoulder. "I'm sure I'll be okay."

16. A JAR OF MUSTARD

"You think she'll be okay?" Kansas asked as Emma helped Francine hobble off to the nurse's office.

Brendan shrugged. "She'll probably hurl," he said.

"Yeah," Andre agreed. "She'll hurl for sure."

"I hope not," Natalie said, shooting worried glances toward the cafeteria door. "Maybe I should go see if she's all right." But she didn't get up.

"She's totally gonna hurl," Brendan replied. "Anyone would barf with eighty-nine packets of ketchup inside them."

"It was eighty-seven," Kansas told him. "And I wouldn't barf."

"Sure you would."

Kansas shook his head. "The only dares that ever make me barf are spinning ones. Like one time Ricky and Will dared me to tie my shoelaces to the center of the merry-go-round at the park, and they spun me around a hundred times as fast as they could. And I totally puked." Luis laughed. "Spinning always makes me puke," Kansas said.

The bell rang, and Brendan rose to his feet. Andre rose too.

"Whatever, *Kansas*," Brendan told him, tossing an empty ketchup packet across the table.

Kansas threw his head back and howled. *"Aaaaaaaah-OOOOOOOH!"*

"Bye, Kansas!" Andre called as he and Brendan left the cafeteria.

"Aaaaaaaah-OOOOOOOH!" Kansas wailed again.

Luis raised his camera to his face and snapped a picture. "Got it!" he told Kansas. "The perfect shot. You're really gonna like that one."

Natalie and Alicia had already left the cafeteria, and Kansas started to leave too, but then he noticed Luis, who was tossing ketchup packets into the garbage. Leave it to Luis to clean up someone else's mess. Kansas glanced at the cafeteria door, where fourth-graders were streaming out in droves, then sighed and turned to help Luis.

"Hey," Luis said, scooping a handful of ketchup packets into the trash, "I meant to tell you. My mom moved my party from Saturday to Sunday. The weekend right after school's out. You think you can come, or is that when you're camping?"

Kansas focused his gaze on a particularly blobby ketchup stain on the table. "Um," he said. Kansas didn't really want to go to Luis's party. It wasn't going to be nearly as fun as camping with Ricky and Will. But what else did he have to do? "Yeah. I mean, I guess I can go."

"Awesome!" Luis said. Kansas did his best to smile.

There was a tap on Kansas's shoulder. Kansas could tell, by the way Luis's face drained completely of color, that whoever was standing behind him was someone he absolutely did *not* want to see.

Slowly, he turned.

It was a large woman with a bulbous nose and

thick-rimmed glasses. She was wearing a suit, one of those lady ones with a skirt, and the fabric pinched at every button. She did not look happy.

"Kansas Bloom?" she said.

Kansas didn't want to, but he had to. He darted his eyes toward Luis, who nodded slowly, his eyes wide with fear. *"Aaaaaaaah-OOOOOOOH!"* Kansas howled. And then he blinked. "Um, yeah," he said. "That's me."

The woman pursed her lips together into one fierce line. "I'm Mrs. Weinmore," she told him. "Your principal."

"Oh," Kansas squeaked. He'd just howled at the *principal*? "Um, hi."

"A little birdie," Mrs. Weinmore continued, studying Kansas's face with angry eyes, "tells me that you've been engaging in *dares*."

"Dares?" Kansas's voice was squeakier than a chipmunk's.

"Yes. *Dares*." Mrs. Weinmore frowned. "Is there any truth to that statement?" Kansas shook his head, whip-fast. "Ah. So then what, may I ask"—Mrs. Weinmore reached into the trash can and pulled out a mound of used ketchup packets—"is all *this*?"

"Um . . . ketchup?"

Mrs. Weinmore shot the ketchup packets back into the garbage. Flecks of red splattered her fingers. "Young man," she spat, "I realize you're new to our school, but let me be the first to tell you that pranks and high jinks will not be tolerated here. Nor," she went on, "are they the way to make girls fall in love with you."

Kansas's eyes went wide. Girls? *Love?* What the heck was she talking about?

"I expect you to be on your very best behavior from now on, do you hear me, Kansas Bloom?"

Kansas nodded. And then, as quietly as he could manage . . .

"Aaaaaaaah-oo—"

Mrs. Weinmore stuck a fat, red finger right in his face. "I'll be keeping a very careful eye on you. Do you understand?"

Kansas nodded. His legs had gone numb. He was pretty sure his *spleen* had gone numb.

"Now," Mrs. Weinmore went on, her face as cold as stone, "why don't the two of you race on back to class before the tardy bell rings, hmm?"

Kansas and Luis didn't need to be told twice.

"Jeez," Kansas whispered as they scuttled down the hallway. "Is she always that scary?"

"Yes," Luis replied quickly. He checked over his shoulder just as they arrived at Miss Sparks's room. "Who do you think ratted you out about the dares?"

That was one question Kansas knew the answer to right away. "Francine," he replied. That sneaky little fink, trying to get him in trouble so she'd win the war. "It was definitely Francine."

The way Ginny was hopping from one foot to another, it either meant she was super excited or that she had to pee.

"We're going to the park!" she sang. "We're going to the park!"

Kansas rolled his eyes at her as she danced her way toward the pick-up spot in front of the school. At least she didn't have to pee, he thought.

"Ginny, calm down. You're making me bonkers."

"Park park park park park!" she sang, still hopping. She was wearing her sparkly tutu again. Now that she knew it had helped Kansas's class win an ice cream party on Friday, she said she wanted to wear it to school every day so she could win ice cream too.

"He's not even here yet," Kansas said. "Why don't you just wait to do all your hopping till he actually picks us up?"

Ginny stopped hopping. "Don't say that. He's coming, and you know it. And then when he lives here, he can take us to the park all the time. You want to see me cartwheel?"

With that, Ginny was halfway down the front lawn, turning hand over face as she attempted one cartwheel after another. It was about as impressive as her headstand.

Kansas was so busy watching Ginny, making sure she didn't break her leg or worse, that he didn't even notice Francine until she was standing right in front of him.

"Kansas Bloom!" she hollered. She didn't look sick anymore, just angry. Kansas had liked her better when she'd been queasy.

Kansas pulled his attention away from his sister. "What do you want?" he growled at Francine.

"Ha!" she cried. "You didn't do it. You were supposed to howl."

"School's over," he replied. "And I already got the point."

Francine stuck her hands on her hips. "Why don't you just give up already?" she said. "You don't even care about Media Club."

"Why don't *you* give up?" Kansas asked. "You don't care about anyone but yourself." Then, because he could, Kansas decided to really get her where it hurt. "You're never going to win anyway. It's five to four. You know you'll never beat me."

Francine was just opening her mouth—to say something obnoxious, most likely—when from across the lawn came the sound of Ginny's voice.

"*Kan*-sas!" she hollered. "*Kan*-SAS! You're not watching me! You gotta watch me cartwheel! I'm going to cartwheel in the talent show and win the prize!"

Kansas whirled around. All he could make out was a sparkly white tumbling blob. "Just a second!" he shouted back to her. "Sheesh!"

"Who's that?" Francine said. "Your lame sister?"

Kansas spun back around. "You leave my sister *alone*," he told her.

"Oh, yeah?" Francine said. "And what if I don—"

Kansas didn't know where the growl came from, but it was fierce. *"MY SISTER KNOWS KUNG FU!"* he bellowed. It was so loud he was pretty sure the entire state heard it. It was loud enough to startle Francine. "You leave her alone," he said again, and then he turned and crossed the lawn to watch Ginny cartwheel.

"You just wait, Kansas Bloom!" Francine hollered at him as he walked away. "I'm going to win, you'll see! You just *wait!*"

Kansas waited awhile, but it wasn't for Francine. Fifteen minutes later, when everyone else had cleared out of the parking lot, Kansas and Ginny were still standing there. Waiting.

"Ginny?" He looked over at her as she swiped at her eyes with the back of her hand. She was done cartwheeling. Kansas sort of wished she'd start again. "I'm sure he's just stuck in traffic or something," he said. "Stay here, okay? I'm going to call him."

Inside the office, Kansas asked if he could use the

telephone. "My dad's late picking me up," he told the secretary. She nodded.

Kansas dialed his dad's new cell phone number, the one he'd given them the day before. The phone rang once, then twice, then three times. Kansas was gearing up to leave a message when his father answered.

"Nicholas Bloom."

"Dad?" Kansas said. "Where are you?"

"Kansas! Hey, champ. I just hit Mount Shasta on I-5. Making good time. How was school?"

"Dad?" All of a sudden Kansas felt a lump in his throat. He'd known it all along, that their dad wasn't going to pick them up, and now his throat had gone *lumpy*? What was his throat going to lump at next? The sky being blue? "You're driving home?"

"Yeah. I was supposed to be at work today." Kansas could hear traffic rushing past on the other end of the line. "The boss is going to be furious. Good seeing you yesterday, though. Sorry I didn't get a chance to say good-bye this morning."

Kansas could see the secretary watching him across the

desk, but her eyes darted away quickly when she noticed him looking. He turned and faced the door. "But you were going to take us to the park," he said, and he knew even as he said it that he sounded pathetic. He could see his own sniveling six-year-old self, crying on the phone three years ago: "But you said . . . you *promised*!" Kansas swallowed hard, but the lump was still there. "Ginny was really excited about it," he said.

"Oh, yeah," his dad replied. "But the park will still be there next time, right? I really have a lot I need to get done this week. Should've driven back last night, really."

"But—"

"Listen, champ, I'd love to chat more, but I'm not supposed to talk on the cell when I'm driving. Wouldn't want your old man to get a ticket, would you? But I'll talk to you soon! Tell Ginny I love her."

Kansas gripped the receiver so hard he could feel his heartbeat in his palm. "Tell her yourself," he said. And he hung up the phone.

When he turned back around, the secretary was looking at him with a slight frown.

"Everything all right?" she asked him.

Kansas wiped his nose. "Yeah," he said. "Yeah. I just . . ." She looked concerned. What right did she have to be *concerned* about him? She didn't even *know* him. "I just got confused. Someone else is supposed to pick me and my sister up."

"Oh." She nodded, but Kansas could tell she didn't believe him. "Okay."

"Can I make another call?"

"Go right ahead."

Kansas's mom was still at work, so Kansas called Mrs. Muñoz, who seemed more than thrilled to pick him and Ginny up from school.

"You got it all worked out?" the secretary asked after he'd hung up, her voice all sugar sweetness.

Kansas pretended he hadn't heard her and shuffled out of the office without saying a word.

"When's he gonna get here?" Ginny said as soon as Kansas reached her. They were the only two people left outside. All the kids were gone; all the cars were gone.

Kansas blinked.

"He's not," he said.

"What do you mean he's not?" Ginny asked. "What did you say to him? Why isn't he coming?"

Because he never comes. That's what Kansas wanted to say. *Because he's the worst dad in the world, and you should just give up on him now and save yourself a lot of trouble.* That was the truth, and if Ginny could just figure it out, she'd be better off in the long run. Kansas had figured it out, and look how well he was doing.

"He . . ." Kansas opened his mouth to say it, but the words wouldn't come. "He had an emergency," he said at last. "At work. He really wanted to come, but he couldn't."

Ginny started crying again then. They weren't the big blubbery tears she usually cried, but silent, sad, gulpy ones. Somehow those seemed worse.

Kansas put a hand on her shoulder and squeezed it—not super tight so she'd think he was actually trying to hug her, but just enough so that maybe he really was. "He"—he took a breath—"he says to say he loves you."

Ginny was silent for a long time, and Kansas just stood there, awkwardly, in his semihug-semipat, praying that every car that passed by the school would belong to Mrs. Muñoz.

Jeez, how slow did she drive anyway?

Ginny pulled away from Kansas and sat down on the curb, her arms cradling the pink Barbie backpack in her lap.

"Ginny?" Kansas sat down next to her, but she didn't look at him. "Ginny?"

When she answered him, her voice was a whisper. "What's kung fu?" she asked.

"Huh?"

"You told that girl I know kung fu. When you were shouting, before."

"Oh." He let out a tiny laugh. "Kung fu's like karate."

Ginny scratched her head. "I don't know how to do it," she told him.

"I know," Kansas said. "I was lying."

"Oh."

Kansas stared at the street a while longer, focusing and unfocusing his eyes so the cars became blurry streaks as they whizzed by.

"Hey, Kansas?"

"Yeah, Gin?"

"Don't lie anymore, 'kay?" she said. She kicked a pebble on the ground in front of her. "I don't like when people lie."

• • •

Kansas was helping Ginny with her homework at the kitchen table when the doorbell rang.

"Subtraction is, like, the easiest thing on earth," he told her for the twelfth time. "You could get it if you tried."

The doorbell rang again.

"You gonna get the door?" Ginny asked, her forehead wrinkled in that way it did when she was in a particularly bad mood. She'd been acting rotten ever since Mrs. Muñoz had driven them home. Kansas didn't see what she was being so terrible to him for. He wasn't the one who ditched them to drive back to Oregon. "Or you gonna be a dumbhead some more?"

"Don't call me a dumbhead," Kansas replied.

"Dumbhead, dumbhead, dumbhead, dumbhead . . ."

Kansas got up to see who was at the door.

It was their mother, holding two armfuls of groceries. "Thanks," she said, pushing past him when he opened the door. "I couldn't get the doorknob. There's three more bags in the car, will you help?"

Kansas grumbled his way out to the driveway and picked through the trunk until he found the lightest bag. "Ginny!"

he hollered as he came back into the kitchen. "Mom said you have to help with the groceries!"

"I'm doing subtraction, dumbhead!" she shouted back at him.

Kansas's mother was putting vegetables into the refrigerator. "How was the park?" she asked him. "And where's your dad? I didn't see his car."

"We didn't go to the park," Kansas told her, setting the bag by the sink. He headed back out the door. Unloading groceries was better than talking to his mother. "And Dad's in Mount Shasta!"

Even from the driveway Kansas could hear his mother's *"What?"*

"What?" she asked again, as soon as he'd walked back in the door. She grabbed the grocery bag from him and set it on the table, right on top of Ginny's subtraction homework.

"Hey!" Ginny hollered.

"Kansas, what do you mean your father's in Mount Shasta? How could he be there already when he just picked you up from school?"

"Well, he's probably not even there anymore," Kansas

said, pulling a box of Fruit Roll-Ups out of the grocery bag and ripping it open. "That was, like, two hours ago. He's probably home by now." He tore open a fruit roll and chomped on a corner, without even bothering to unroll it all the way.

"Kansas, dinner's in a half hour," his mother said. But she just watched him eat the fruit roll, didn't grab it from him like she normally would have. "And what are you talking about?"

"Daddy didn't take us to the stupid park," Ginny said, shoving the paper bag off her homework. "He didn't pick us up. We missed the bus, so Mrs. Muñoz had to get us."

"What?" Kansas's mom asked. Ginny was still shoving the grocery bag. "Where's Mrs. Muñoz now? Is she here?"

"She had to go home to start dinner," Kansas told her. "But she's right next door, and anyway me and Ginny can take care of ourselves."

"But what if something had happened?" his mother said. She was wiping her bangs across her forehead, looking totally freaked out. "Why didn't you call me at work? Why didn't you *tell* me your dad didn't show up? Ginny, will you stop messing with the groceries?"

"They're on top of my homework!"

Kansas gritted his teeth. "We didn't call you," he told his mom, "because it wasn't exactly a big news story. So Dad didn't show up? So wh—"

There was a sharp *crack!* of glass, and all at once Kansas's nose was filled with the overwhelming smell of mustard.

Ginny had knocked the grocery bag off the table.

"Ginny!" their mother shouted. "For the love of God! Will you just pay attention for three seconds to what you're . . ." She trailed off as she ripped open a new roll of paper towels. She knelt down to peer inside the bag. "Oh, God, now the whole bag's full of mustard. This was our *dinner*. And I have class in an hour. Kansas, don't just stand there, get some towels."

"What did *I* do?" Kansas whined. "Ginny's the moron who—"

"I'm not a moron!" Ginny screeched.

Oh, good, now Ginny had gone and started *crying*.

"Kansas, stop yelling at your sister and help me over

166

here." His mom was pulling groceries out of the bag, her jeans smothered in yellow goop. "Can't you two just get along for thirty sec—"

"*I'm* not the one *yelling!*" Kansas yelled. "Get mad at *her!*" He shot a finger at Ginny, who was wailing in her chair, the heels of her hands smearing tears across her face. "This whole family is full of morons."

"Kansas!" his mom cried. "Go to your room!"

"Already going!" Kansas replied, stomping down the hallway. He made sure each of his footsteps was nice and loud, and when he got to his and Ginny's bedroom, he slammed the door. And then, because he wasn't sure he'd slammed it hard enough the first time, he slammed it again. He kicked at the wall of boxes in the center of the room as he passed it, and then watched in horror as it—*crunch, crinkle, crumble*—crashed to the ground.

Kansas plopped face-first onto his bed.

There were a million thoughts buzzing around in his head, all of them angry and mean. *Stupid Ginny messing up the stupid cardboard wall. Stupid Mom for stupid yelling at him when he didn't even DO anything.*

But the loudest thought of all, the angriest and meanest, was the one thought Kansas wished he wasn't thinking.

No wonder his dad left them. No wonder he never wanted to be around them. This whole family stank.

He looked up at the Wall of Dares, all those photos of things he'd done with his very best friends in the world—the friends who had up and forgotten about him the second he'd moved away. Maybe it wasn't his family that stank, Kansas thought. Maybe it was just him.

He reached up an arm and, one by one, yanked the photos off the wall.

"Kansas!" his mother hollered from out in the hallway. "Come on, we have to go back to the grocery store before my night class!"

"You just sent me to my *room*!" Kansas shouted back. But he picked himself off the bed anyway, kicking the ruined cardboard wall. On his way out the door, he stuffed the photos into the garbage.

168

17.

A bag of jumbo marshmallows

Francine wanted to hate her bedroom in her dad's new apartment—wanted to despise everything about it, on principle. But there was one part of the room that she found she actually liked quite a bit. In one corner, by the light switch, there was a bookcase built right into the wall. It was skinny and tall, with shelves all the way to the ceiling, and the first shelf started two feet off the ground. There was just enough space underneath for Francine to fold herself inside, knees drawn in close to her chest. Sitting there made Francine feel calm, like she was just another story tucked inside a bookcase.

She was sitting there on Tuesday morning, before they were supposed to leave for school, when her father poked his head into the room. "Well, you seem to have made yourself right at home," he said with a small smile. He looked around. There was nothing in the room yet, really. Just a duffel bag full of clothes and Francine's old camping sleeping bag scrunched in the corner like a pile of dirty laundry. "We need to get you some furniture. Why don't we go on Thursday, after school? We can get you a dresser and a desk, and we can pick out some new beds."

Francine crawled out of the bookcase. "I don't need a bed," she said. "I have one at home."

"This is your home now too, you know. And you can't sleep in a sleeping bag for the rest of your life."

Francine sighed and walked out into the hallway.

"Pea pod?" her father called. "Where are you going?"

"I have to pee!" she shouted back.

Francine did not have to pee. But the bathroom was the one place in the apartment that didn't look like an empty cave. It was the one place that didn't look like it was the start of a brand-new life. So that's where she went.

•   •   •

Twenty minutes later, Francine and her father had just pulled out of the driveway to go to Media Club, when Francine spotted something that she absolutely did *not* want to see.

Kansas Bloom.

He was waiting at the bus stop across the street. Behind him, she could make out the frill of a sparkly white tutu, which must be his idiot little sister. Francine scrunched down low in her seat, head ducked below the window. So Kansas was her *neighbor* now? Great. Just great. What if he saw her? What if he figured out that her dad had just moved there? What if he found out about her parents?

Her father coughed a tiny cough. "Pea pod?" he said. "You sick or something?"

"Huh?" Francine peeked her head over the edge of the window. Kansas and the bus stop were well out of sight. She tucked a strand of green hair behind her ear. She'd slept in the braids two nights in a row, and they were now mostly a mash of green matted hair on top of her head, a few bobby pins poking out here and there. Not Francine's greatest look. "I'm fine," she said, inching her butt back into her seat. "I was just adjusting my socks."

"Well, let's hope they stay up for the rest of the school day, huh?" her father said. And he laughed, even though, really, there was nothing to laugh about at all.

As soon as Francine got to Media Club, everyone voted on her dare for the day. She had to stick jumbo marshmallows onto herself—an entire bag—and spend all of first recess pretending to be some sort of "marshmallow monster." It was Emma's idea. She'd brought the bag of marshmallows and everything.

Alicia was the one who came up with Kansas's dare. He had to duct tape an ice cube to the crook of his arm until it melted. The club voted, and they all agreed.

So, when recess rolled around, Francine found herself licking the sides of 32 jumbo marshmallows and sticking them to her skin. She had marshmallows on her hands, marshmallows on her cheeks, marshmallows on her neck, even marshmallows balanced on top of her green hair. Her tongue was sticky with melted sugar, and her front teeth felt fuzzy. She was getting pretty sick of food dares.

Still, she seemed better off than Kansas, who was squirming next to her on the bench. The duct tape was pulling at the arm hairs below his T-shirt, as the icy water dribbled out from underneath it.

Francine stuck two marshmallows to her forehead.

Kansas shook with cold, gritting his teeth as Alicia patted the duct tape against the inside of his elbow to see if the ice cube had fully melted yet.

Francine plopped the last marshmallow into her mouth and stood up on the bench. She growled at two passing third-graders. "I'm the marshmallow monster of the fourth grade!" she declared, stretching out her marshmallowy hands at them. The two kids screeched and ran off.

Emma began to cheer, but Brendan just scowled and said, "I *told* you guys Francine's dare was too easy."

But no one was paying him any attention, because at that moment Alicia announced that Kansas's ice cube was completely melted, and the group broke into applause.

Francine felt a little better when Alicia ripped the duct tape off and Kansas squealed like a baby. But she felt a little worse when Natalie rushed to his side to make sure he was okay, twirling a lock of her hair as she fawned over him.

When the bell rang, Francine peeled off the marshmallows and tossed them in the garbage. Then she walked back to room 43H all by herself, sticking to every single thing she passed.

The score was five to six.

On Wednesday, Francine had to write a love letter to Mr. DuPree. She told him he was a handsome dresser and that she fainted every time she thought about him. The members of the Media Club all watched as she slipped it into his mailbox in the front office.

Mr. DuPree did not respond.

Kansas's dare was to try out for the girls' volleyball team during lunch. The members of the Media Club peered around the gym door as he ran drills and spiked balls. Twice he accidentally walloped Emma in the face.

He did not make the team.

At the end of the day, the score was six to seven. Kansas was still in the lead, with only a week and a half left before winter break.

• • •

On Thursday, Francine had to wear a sign safety-pinned to her shirt all day that read MAJOR DOOFUS. Kansas's dare was that he wasn't allowed to speak, no matter what anyone said to him. Finally, a dare Francine could support.

During literature, the last period of the day, when Miss Sparks asked if anyone wanted to read the poem they'd written for homework, Brendan raised his hand.

"Great, Brendan," Miss Sparks said. "Why don't you come up to the front of the class?"

"Oh, I don't want to read mine," he said. "I was just going to say that I think Kansas wants to do it. He wrote a really good one. He was reading it to me at lunch, weren't you, Kansas? But he's sort of shy. That's why he didn't raise his own hand."

Even from across the room, Francine could see the silent death glare Kansas shot at Brendan.

"Wonderful. Kansas, I'm sure we'd all love to hear what you've written."

Kansas shook his head slowly.

"Ask him *why* he won't read it," Brendan piped up.

"Kansas?" Miss Sparks asked. "Is everything okay?

You seem a little . . . quiet today." Kansas remained silent. "Well, all right." She looked around the room. "Is there anyone else who would like to read?"

From behind her, Francine heard a whispered, "Major Doofus!" and then there was a sudden pinch at her elbow. Her hand shot up in the air, and she whirled around to glare at Andre, who smirked.

"Francine?" Miss Sparks asked. "Are you volunteering?"

Francine turned back around. "Sure," she said with a sigh. Why not? She walked to the front of the room, smoothing the MAJOR DOOFUS sign across her chest, to read her poem. Luckily it was only four lines long.

On her way back to her seat, Natalie slipped a note into her hand. It wasn't folded into a heart or a star or anything fancy. It was just a regular rectangle. Francine waited until she got back to her desk and then smoothed out the creases to read it.

> **I forgot to tell you I can't come over today because I'm going to Alicia's after school.**
> **—Natalie**

Francine shoved the note into her desk. She didn't know why her stomach was feeling so bubbly and squirmy all of a sudden. Almost like she was upset. What did she have to be upset about? It wasn't like Natalie could've come over that afternoon anyway. That afternoon Francine and her dad were going furniture shopping.

After the bell rang, Francine unpinned the MAJOR DOOFUS sign from her shirt and walked to the front of the class to throw it away as all the other kids streamed out of the room.

Miss Sparks looked up from her desk. "I'd think you'd be a colonel, at least," she said, eyes resting on the sign at the top of the trash can.

"Huh?" Francine asked. Miss Sparks smiled and shook her head slightly. Francine shrugged, then erased the six on her corner of the board and changed it to a seven. Kansas had already written in his eight. At this rate, she'd never win.

There were over two hundred different kinds of mattresses at Mattress King—that's what the sign said out front. Francine flopped down on one labeled "100% Memory

Foam" and called to her father four mattresses away, "I thought you said we could get sundaes!" They'd been furniture shopping for two hours already, and Francine was pooped.

Her father walked across the store and sat down on the mattress Francine was on. "Right after this," he said, bobbing up and down on it a little to get a feel for it. "I promise."

"Can't we just go now?"

"I need to get a mattress first. Sleeping on the floor is rough at my age. And you need a real bed too." He leaned back onto the mattress, his feet still flat on the floor and his hands folded over his stomach. "This one's not bad, right?"

Francine looked straight up at the ceiling. When her voice came out, it was so ribbon-thin, Francine wondered for a moment if it was even hers. "Can't you just come home?" she asked.

"Francine," her father said. "Pea pod." Francine turned to look at him, and he patted the mattress between them. "String cheese time," he told her.

Francine bit her bottom lip. She did not want to laugh.

"Come on," he said, coaxing. "String cheese!" He scooted up on the mattress until only his feet were hanging off. "I can't do it by myself, you know."

When Francine had been super little, four or five maybe, she used to come into the living room when her dad was stretched out on the couch watching TV, and she'd lie down flat right next to him, squeezed in tight so she wouldn't fall off the side. It used to be one of her favorite things to do, squeeze next to her dad on the couch and stay like that, watching soccer or the news or stupid alien movies on TV. Her dad said they must look so silly, like one long stick of string cheese. It got so every time the TV came on, they'd both shout "string cheese!" and race to the couch to see who could get there first.

Her father raised an eyebrow at her, the right one.

Francine sniffled up the tears that had been threatening to come out, wiped her nose, and laughed. Then she scooted up parallel to her dad, her side squeezed up tight against his, and her arms straight at her sides just like his were. "String cheese," she said.

"String cheese!" they both shouted together. A couple at the end of the store looked over at them, and they both burst into giggles.

"Look," her father said after a good minute of string cheesing. "I'm in my own place for good now. I am. And I think you know that."

"But what if . . . ?" Francine ran through all the *Parent Trap* scenarios in her head. What if her parents met up again on a yacht? What if they were forced to spend more time together? Then wouldn't they fall back in love? Francine just needed to figure out exactly what to do to make it happen. "What if you change your mind?" she said at last.

Her father offered her a sad sort of smile. "I won't," he said. "I'm sorry, pea pod. I know that's not what you want to hear. But your mother and I are getting a divorce."

Suddenly Francine didn't want to string cheese anymore. She sat up and pulled herself off the mattress, wandering over to another aisle.

"Francine!" Her father got up and followed her.

"You should get this one," she told him, pointing to the

mattress in front of her. "I mean, it's pink and everything, but you'd never know when you put the sheets on it."

"Francine," her father said again.

"And it's on sale."

"Francine."

Why did he think that if he just said her name a whole bunch, everything would be okay? It wouldn't be okay. They were shopping for mattresses, for goodness' sake. Nothing would ever be okay again. She spun around on her heel and glared at him. "I want my ice cream sundae now," she said.

"Francine, listen to me."

"No."

"*Francine.*" He picked her up and set her—*plop!*—on top of the pink mattress, and he took hold of both of her hands. She wiggled free of him, but he grabbed her hands again and held on until she finally looked at him. "Francine," he said. "You're a smart girl. And I know that this is hard on you, and I'm sorry. I'm so sorry, Francine. But I think, in the end, it really is the best thing we can do for you, to give you two happy parents, instead of two just sort-of-fine ones."

"But . . ." Francine sniffled. "We were happy." She looked down at the stitching on the mattress, the way the lines crossed each other, breaking the surface up into perfect diamonds. "I thought we were happy before."

Her father took a moment to think about that. He let go of her hands and sat down next to her, but he didn't talk, not for a long time. Then, finally, he said, "We were, mostly." He paused and smoothed his hand across the top of her hair then, the way he used to when she was little. "But I don't think there's just one kind of happiness. You and I and your mother, I think we need to find a different way to be happy." He tucked a loose strand of green hair behind her ear. "Does that make sense, pea pod?"

Francine fingered the stitching on the mattress, letting the words sink in. *A different way to be happy.* Was it possible to be happy with two different houses, two different beds?

"Maybe," she said. She puffed out her cheeks. "I guess."

"You ready for ice cream?"

"But I thought . . ." Francine looked around at the hundreds of mattresses.

"I can sleep on the floor a few more days before my back gives out, I think. What I *really* need right now is some rocky road. What do you say?"

At that, Francine gave him the tiniest smile. "With hot fudge," she said.

18. A BLUE SWIVELY CHAIR

Kansas was in for a surprise when he arrived at Media Club on Friday morning.

"Club members," Miss Sparks announced, "Alicia won't be here for the announcements today. Her father just called, and she has an early dentist's appointment. So I've decided that this morning we will have both Kansas and Francine try out the news anchor's desk."

Kansas was so busy watching Brendan slap his desk that it took him a moment to register what Miss Sparks had just said. News anchor? Him? *Today?*

Miss Sparks smiled at both Kansas and Francine in turn.

"It will be good practice for whichever one of you ends up with the job. So!" She clapped her hands. "We have a lot of work to do, don't you think? Let's get bustling!"

And what a lot of bustling there was. While everyone else went about their normal jobs, Kansas and Francine got set up behind the desk. Francine grabbed Miss Sparks's big blue swively chair before Kansas even had a chance to say he wanted it, but Brendan and Andre helpfully offered to borrow one from Mr. Paulsen next door so that Kansas could have a nice, big, twirling one too. Once he was seated, he and Francine began splitting up the announcements.

"Do you want to read this one?" Kansas asked Francine, flipping through the papers. "About the talent show?" He wanted to give her all the ones with words he wasn't sure how to pronounce.

But Francine wasn't paying attention. "Emma!" she hollered, jumping out of her chair so quickly it toppled over. "That's not how you turn on the camera! No, it's not *that* button, it's . . . Here, let me show you."

While Francine taught Emma how to use the camera, Natalie came over to make Kansas "camera ready." This mostly consisted of pushing the hair on top of his head from one side to the other.

"You sure you don't want any lip gloss?" she asked.

"Uh, no."

"But it'll make your lips shinier."

Kansas told Natalie that he was perfectly happy with his unshiny lips, thank you.

After the bell rang and the other students in Miss Sparks's class began to trickle in and take their seats, Francine finally came back to sit beside Kansas. But she didn't stay long.

"Emma, no!" she hollered again. "I *told* you! That's not how you zoom!"

Kansas shook his head and turned his focus to the papers in front of him, reading each one over carefully so he'd be sure to say everything correctly. His palms were itchy. He'd never been on camera before. What if he did something embarrassing?

"Two minutes!" Miss Sparks called.

Luis came back into the room and handed the last-minute announcements to Brendan, who looked at them quickly, then began scribbling notes on top. Francine returned to the news desk so Natalie could prep her, but after squinting at her for ten seconds, Natalie announced that there was "nothing to do for green hair," and wandered off. Francine scowled into her stack of papers. Kansas did his best to ignore her. He'd rather share a news desk with a warthog.

The bell rang.

"Places, everyone!" Emma shouted, clearly enjoying her new role behind the camera. Kansas ran his tongue over his teeth, checking to make sure he didn't have any leftover oatmeal stuck there. Beside him, Francine sat up a little straighter. For someone who'd been trying to be news anchor so badly, Kansas thought, she looked downright petrified. Kansas smiled.

"Ten seconds!" Emma hollered.

That's when Kansas noticed Andre, walking right toward him.

"Is something wrong?" Kansas asked. "Is there a problem with the lights?"

Andre placed the stack of last-minute announcement on

top of Kansas's pile of papers. But he didn't answer his question. He turned, instead, to Francine. "We double dog dare you . . . ," Andre began.

"And five!" Emma screeched.

". . . to pick your nose . . ."

"Four!"

". . . on camera . . ."

"Three!"

". . . and . . ."

"Two!"

". . . eat it."

"ROLLING!"

Andre turned and raced away. The light on the camera turned green.

Francine was speechless. She sat, staring at the camera, her mouth hanging open. It was hard to tell if she had stage fright or was still in shock about the dare. Maybe a little of both.

But Kansas, surprisingly, found that he felt cool as a cucumber.

"Good morning, Auden Elementary," he said, smiling

into the camera. He turned his focus away from Francine and thought instead about what he was supposed to say. "Happy Friday. Alicia's out sick, so Francine and I are going to be your co–news anchors for the day." This wasn't so bad. Nope, not at all. "I'm Kansas Bloom." He turned to Francine.

"Um . . . ," Francine said slowly. Her hands were shaking on top of the desk, and her face, Kansas couldn't help noticing, was almost as green as her hair. Was she going to do it? Would she really do the dare?

Slowly, Francine raised her hand to her face.

She *wouldn't,* Kansas thought. Not in front of the whole school.

She reached one outstretched finger to her nose.

No *way.*

She took a deep breath . . .

And, just like that, Francine Halata picked her nose.

And ate it.

The room exploded with shouts and screams and laughter. The whole *school* exploded. You could hear it out the door, echoing down the hallway.

Wow, Kansas thought. That had actually been sort of impressive.

At the far end of the room, Miss Sparks had her lips drawn into a tight line. It wasn't a frown, but it definitely wasn't a smile either. Kansas waited until the ruckus around him had died down to a low rumble, and then he looked at the stack of the papers in front of him, to start reading the announcements.

But what was on top of Kansas's papers wasn't an announcement.

It was a note, on a small scrap of paper, written in Brendan's pointy, thin scrawl.

We double dog dare you to spin around in your chair for the entire announcements.

Kansas gulped. Spinning was the one thing he wasn't good at.

But a dare was a dare.

Without a further second of hesitation, Kansas picked up his stack of announcements, tucked his toes to the ground, and spun himself around in his swively chair.

"The PTA is having a bake sale!" he announced as he twirled. One twirl, two twirls, threefourfivesix . . . His brain was already a jumble of dizziness, but he wouldn't stop. He *couldn't.* "Next Friday, before the winter talent show." Eleven twirls. Twelve. The dippy bird perched on the edge of the desk was a blur of red and blue. Thirteen. Fourteen . . . Kansas lost count. Every time his eyes whirled past Miss Sparks, he could see her shaking her head into her hands, but still Kansas kept spinning. "Fifty cents for cupcakes, a quarter for cookies. Francine, over to you."

"Uh . . ." Even now that she was done with her dare, Francine's voice sounded trembly. She looked down at her own stack of papers. "Congratulations to Dylan Kutner for winning the spelling bee last night. Dylan will be competing in the semifinals next month, so everybody wish him luck. Kansas, back to you."

Was it Kansas's turn to talk again already? He took a deep breath and, stomach beginning to churn like a dishwasher, he read from his sheet of paper.

"The school talent show is coming up next—"

Kansas's stomach gave a threatening lurch. But still he kept spinning. Spinning and reading.

"The talent show is next Fri—"

A sour tang crept into the back of his throat. But still he continued to spin.

"Friday. The show is next Friday. Come watch your schoolmates compete in all sorts of acts. The winning act will get two hundred—"

Kansas tried to stop it. He really did.

But there, in front of the camera . . .

. . . in front of the school . . .

. . . his vision shifted into sparks and darkness . . .

. . . and, still spinning . . .

. . . Kansas Bloom barfed up his breakfast. Bananas and oatmeal, and a glass of OJ. It all came out in a spin, spewed on the desk, on the ground, all around him in a perfect circle.

Kansas stopped spinning and looked over at Francine, his head barely lifted off his chest. He had never felt so miserable. Pukey and miserable. He was never going to live this down. He couldn't say that he was the King of Dares, not anymore. He hadn't finished the dare, so he hadn't gotten the point, and now they were tied, eight to eight. And the tiny part of him that felt anything other than pure and utter *awful* was plain angry, because he knew—*knew*—that Francine was going to be so, so happy.

But Francine didn't look happy.

Actually, she looked like she might . . .

19.

A dippy bird

Barf.

That was the only word running through Francine's head.

There was barf everywhere. Barf on her shoes, barf all over the floor, even a little bit flecked on her jeans. And in the glass in front of Miss Sparks's dippy bird, was that . . . ? Yes. It was oatmeal. Kansas had eaten oatmeal for breakfast, Francine could tell for a fact. And now the dippy bird was dunking down to *eat* it.

Her cheeks went hot.

Her forehead went cold.

Her chest pulsed.

Her eyes watered.

And then, in front of the camera, the school, and everybody . . .

Francine barfed too.

20. A DESK FAN

"Well, now," Mrs. Weinmore said, inspecting both Kansas and Francine carefully over the bulb of her nose. "I had a feeling you would both wind up here sooner or later."

Kansas looked up at the clock on Mrs. Weinmore's wall. Eight sixteen. Straight from the nurse to the principal's office in eight minutes flat. That had to be some kind of record.

"Mrs. Weinmore," he began. He could still see a little bit of puke on the toe of his shoe. "It wasn't my fault. I promise. I—"

The principal held up a hand to quiet him. "Mr. Bloom," she said, her voice sharp as an ice pick, "I strongly suggest you stop talking for the time being."

Kansas followed her suggestion.

"I was very clear to both of you," the principal went on, "that no shenanigans would be tolerated in this school. Wasn't I?" She looked first at Francine, then at Kansas, and Kansas could feel her eyes boring into him like lasers. "Wasn't I clear?"

"Yes, ma'am," Kansas mumbled, eyes in his lap, just as Francine squeaked out a "yeah." Mrs. Weinmore's desk fan was pointed straight at him, drying out his eyes with a *whirr.* He wondered if that was part of his punishment.

"I *thought* that I was clear. And yet you both went and made fools of yourselves anyway, in front of the entire student body. *Dares.*" She spat out the word as though it left a rotten taste in her mouth. "If someone told you two to march off a cliff, you'd both do it in a heartbeat. I've never seen such behavior. I know crushes at this age can be overwhelming, but engaging in *dares* is no way to deal with your feelings."

A *crush*? On *Francine*? If Kansas had had anything left in him to barf, he would've upchucked it right there in the principal's office.

Next to Kansas, Francine squirmed in her chair. "You

can't prove we did any dares," she said. "I just had a booger this morning, that's all."

Kansas liked where this was going. "Yeah," he said. "Francine eats her boogers all the time."

Francine nodded furiously. "I do. It's true."

"And me," Kansas added, "I just felt like spin—"

"*Mr.* Bloom. *Miss* Halata." The principal's voice had changed from ice pick to sledge hammer. "Our janitor, Mr. Grell, informs me that he found a small slip of paper on Miss Sparks's desk, underneath your other . . . digestibles. Now, I don't believe there is a single person on this earth who wants to attempt to read what is on that paper. But I am willing to bet that on it there may very well be written a *dare*." For someone with such a bulge of a nose, Kansas thought, Mrs. Weinmore really knew how to look threatening. "If I am forced to read the paper instead of having you tell me what it says directly, I will gladly double your punishment. So, do tell me." She leaned forward on both elbows. "*Was* it a dare, Miss Halata? Mr. Bloom?"

Francine sighed. "Yes," she admitted. "It was a dare." And all Kansas could do was nod in agreement.

"I see. And what do you think might be a suitable punishment for such an offense?"

Kansas was just about to mumble out "getting detention," when suddenly he realized something.

"All I did was *spin,*" he said. So he'd spun around in a chair during the announcements. So what? Was that really worth getting in trouble for? "And that's not against the rules. I mean . . . it's not, right?"

"Yeah," Francine agreed from the seat next to him. Kansas snapped his head in her direction, and he could tell that she felt just as surprised as he did to find them both on the same side. "It's not against the rules to pick your nose, either. If it was, Andre would be in trouble all the time."

The look Mrs. Weinmore shot them then could've shriveled a plum to a prune in three seconds flat. "The two of you," she admonished, "cannot even *begin* to understand the chaos your little morning high jinks have wreaked in this school."

"Um . . . chaos?" Kansas said.

"All across the school"—Mrs. Weinmore swept her arms out to her sides wildly—"we had some of our more . . .

delicate students become ill from watching your little capers on the air."

"Ill?" Francine asked.

"It seems that there can be something of a chain reaction in watching a person vomit." She closed her eyes for a moment in disgust. "Forty-three students," she told them. "Forty-three students are currently in the nurse's office, calling their parents to come pick them up from school."

So *that* was why there had been such a crowd in the nurse's office. Kansas had figured there'd been a lice outbreak or something.

Francine's eyebrows were raised to the ceiling. "You mean, we made forty-three kids . . . ?"

Mrs. Weinmore nodded. "You made forty-three students vomit before first recess," she confirmed. "Forty-five if you include yourselves."

Now *that* had to be a record.

"Which is why," the principal went on, "both of you will be suspended for the rest of the day."

"Suspended?" Kansas's throat felt like it might close up.

He'd never been in trouble in his whole life. He'd never even been to the principal's office before.

"Suspended," Mrs. Weinmore confirmed.

Francine's face went completely pale. "What about . . ." She took a deep breath. "What about Media Club? You're not going to . . . We can still be in it, right?"

Mrs. Weinmore drummed her fingers on the table, studying Francine's face for a long moment. Kansas sank as far back in his chair as possible, as though maybe, if he stayed far enough out of her way, the principal would forget he was there altogether.

"Under normal circumstances, Miss Halata," Mrs. Weinmore replied at last, "I would remove the two of you from Media Club immediately. However, it seems that in this instance I don't have to."

Francine cleared her throat. "Re-really?"

"Really," Mrs. Weinmore replied. "Because as of this coming Monday, Media Club will be canceled."

"What?" Kansas and Francine cried together.

Mrs. Weinmore had already turned her attention to some papers on her desk. "Yes. As it happens, you need a camera to run a media club, and the one you've been using is broken." She tapped the bottom of a stack of papers against her desktop. "It seems that modern-day camera equipment is ill-equipped to handle the effects of vomit."

"Someone vomited on the camera?" Kansas said, his nose wrinkled in disgust. "But me and Francine were too far away. We couldn't have—"

"Emma Finewitz," the principal told him, turning back to her papers once and for all, "was number forty-five."

21.

A sketchbook

What happened when you got suspended at 8:16 on a Friday morning, Francine discovered, was that you had to go to your dad's morning art class, and the whole way there, he wouldn't even look at you or call you "pea pod," and every time you tried to talk to him, he'd just frown and say, "We'll discuss it later, all right, Francine?"

All through her dad's never-ending slideshow about the Impressionist art movement, Francine shifted in her seat in the last row, trying to get comfortable. She didn't understand how college students could sit at such teeny-tiny desks. Her desk at school was at least three times as big, and she was only in fourth grade. She studied the graffiti that had been carved into her desktop. *JB♥CL. JB♥TK. JB♥IN.* And then, the most perplexing, one large scrawl that simply read *ROCKETSHIP.*

Francine scooped her father's sketchbook out of the book bag he'd left beside her desk and flipped through it to see if he'd been working on anything new. Sure enough, near the very end, there was a new machine. This one involved dominoes and bike tires, a sprinkler system, hammers and seltzer bottles, and three cantaloupes. At the very end, a string yanked on a fork to turn on a light switch. Francine stuck her nose right down into the sketchbook, counting. Thirty-seven steps.

Suddenly Francine snapped the sketchbook closed with such a thud that her father frowned at her from the front of the room.

Thirty-seven steps. Thirty-seven steps, all to do something that in the end might not even work anyway.

Francine sank down low in the tiny metal desk chair. It was all so pointless, she realized. Nothing seemed to really matter anymore. Not her father's machines—because they were never going to build one for real, even if her dad kept promising they would. Not Samson training—because he'd never be able to do anything more than crawl straight forward and squeak. Not even the dare war—because Media Club was canceled, so who cared who won? All the plans Francine had ever made, all the steps for her life she'd spent so long plotting out in great detail, were as meaningless as the pen strokes in her dad's sketchbook. Things never worked out the way you planned them. There were always hitches in the middle, problems you didn't see coming. So what was the use in even trying?

That evening, Francine called Natalie's house. She needed someone to talk to, her best friend, and she figured maybe it was finally time to tell Natalie about her parents. But Natalie's mother informed Francine that Natalie was at Alicia's house. She'd be spending the whole weekend there, she said. Would Francine like to leave a message?

"No," Francine said. "Thank you." And she hung up the phone.

22. A TENNIS BALL

What happened when you got suspended at 8:16 on a Friday morning, Kansas discovered, was that your mother had to leave her shift at the gift shop to pick you up at school, and the whole car ride home she yelled at you and lectured and wondered how you could possibly get yourself in trouble at a school you'd only been attending for three weeks. And then, just as you were about to defend yourself, she told you that you were becoming more and more like your father every day, and that you better get your act together, young man, or God help you.

"But—" Kansas tried to protest.

"I don't even want to hear it, Kansas."

Kansas's mom said no computer, no video games, no TV.

206

If he really wanted to be useful, she told him, he could clean up the mess of broken boxes in his and Ginny's room that had been sitting there for the past four days. So Kansas spent most of the day lying on the floor of his bedroom in front of the boxes and not cleaning them up at all, staring at the toys and books and sweaters that had spewed out everywhere. The only things that were left of their old life.

Kansas opened the front door and poked his head outside, checking the Muñozes' house next door. The night was crisp and dark, just a few stars in the sky, but Kansas could still make out the basketball hoop.

He poked his head back inside and shut the door.

Then he opened the door again.

And shut it.

"What the heck are you doing?"

Kansas whirled around and glared at Ginny, standing there in her tutu with her hands on her hips. "Nothing," he said. "Leave me alone."

"If you wanna go out there and play with the basketball hoop, you can, you know. Mr. Muñoz said you could go over whenever you want."

"That's not even what I'm looking at. Like you know everything. For your information I was checking the weather."

"Then why are you holding your basketball?"

"Shut up," Kansas told her.

"At least I'm not afraid of a basketball hoop," Ginny replied. And she leapt back into the living room, doing her best ballerina twirl.

Kansas wasn't afraid of a basketball hoop. It was just sort of weird to go shoot hoops in an old person's driveway. Even if that old person already told you that you could.

Kansas gripped the ball tight against his left hip and opened the door again. After a full day squashed up in his room doing nothing, he decided, he needed to go outside.

He'd made eight free throws in a row when Mr. Muñoz stepped out of his front door. "Hoop looks nice there, doesn't it?" he said.

"Yeah." Kansas shot again into the darkness and—swish!—nothing but net.

"You're pretty good, you know that?" Mr. Muñoz said, hands in his pockets. "Your dad teach you?"

The ball bounced back toward Kansas, and he retrieved it, dribbling a few times as he crossed the driveway. Then he lined up another shot and—*swish!*—sank it again.

Mr. Muñoz watched silently while Kansas made three more perfect shots. He just stood there, watching. Kansas figured he must be pretty bored, if all he had to do was watch some kid shoot hoops in his driveway.

Kansas missed the next shot. The ball went wonky, shooting off the rim and hitting the ground without a bounce. It rolled across the driveway, where it landed at Mr. Muñoz's feet. He picked it up.

"I was never much of an athlete myself," Mr. Muñoz said, juggling the ball in his hands a bit as though he were testing its weight. "Always better with mechanics, things like that." He shot the ball toward the hoop, but Kansas could tell, even before the ball left his hands, that it wasn't going to make it. His grip was too loose, his angle too high.

The ball was short by four feet. Kansas caught it and dribbled it back to the leaf he'd been using as his three-point line. He shot again and scored.

"You should join the basketball team at your school,"

Mr. Muñoz said. "With talent like yours, I'm sure you'd be a shoo-in."

Kansas shot another three-pointer. "There's a club," he replied. Now that Kansas thought about it, he supposed he *could* join basketball, with Media Club canceled and everything. But . . . "I don't really feel like it, though."

"Oh?" Kansas could almost *feel* Mr. Muñoz raising an eyebrow. "Why's that?"

Kansas just shrugged. He didn't know how to explain it. How every time he sank a basket, it reminded him just a little bit of his dad. How even though he loved playing basketball—and knew he was good at it—he hated it just a little bit too. How he wasn't sure if the hate part would ever go away.

"I don't know," he told Mr. Muñoz.

Mr. Muñoz was quiet after that, just watching Kansas sink baskets. But after a while he said, "You know, I've been working on a new project lately. Thought you might be interested in helping me this weekend. I could teach you how to use the power saw."

Kansas shot again. "No, thanks," he said. *Swish!* "I'm

pretty busy. Homework and stuff." He retrieved the ball and aimed again.

Shoot and *swish!*

"Well," Mr. Muñoz said, "anyway. Let me know if you change your mind."

"'Kay," Kansas said. He shot again.

"Have a good night, Kansas."

With that, Mr. Muñoz stepped inside the house and shut the door.

Kansas stayed outside, shooting and *swish*ing, until the lights went out in the Muñozes' house thirty minutes later. Then he tucked the ball under his arm and crossed the driveway back to his own house.

Saturday afternoon, Kansas sat in his room bouncing a dirty tennis ball against the wall, trying to ignore the music from the dumb girly movie that Ginny was blasting from the living room. He'd woken up early that morning to try out the basketball hoop, but even at seven thirty, Mr. Muñoz had been out there, working in the garage with the door open. He asked Kansas if he wanted to play a game of

HORSE with him, and Kansas had lied and said that he had just gone out to get the mail. Then he scuttled back inside the house without even remembering to check the mailbox.

Brilliant.

From the living room, Ginny turned the volume on the TV up, and Kansas responded by throwing the ball even harder, chucking it against the wall with a steady *thud thud thud*.

Thud, thud, THWACK.

Ginny turned the volume up so loud that Kansas could have sworn the television was inside his brain.

"Ginny!" he hollered, snatching up his tennis ball and storming into the living room. "Can you turn that thing down?"

She stuck her tongue out at him without bothering to take her eyes off the screen. "Stop making so much noise so I can hear it."

Kansas looked at the TV. Two girls were wearing camp clothes, hanging up photos in a log cabin during a rainstorm. "Why would you even want to watch this?" he asked his sister. "It looks like the stupidest movie ever."

"Is not," Ginny said. "It's good. It's *The Parent Trap*. These two girls are twins, and their parents get divorced, and they're gonna try to fix it. Franny from yoga said it was really good. I want to see how it ends."

Kansas frowned. He didn't care what some old lady from Ginny's yoga class had said. He recognized the movie now. He'd watched it before, when he was just Ginny's age, right after their father left the first time. And he knew exactly how it ended.

Kansas dropped his tennis ball, stormed over to the TV, and punched the power button. The image on the screen flashed bright white for a split second, then disappeared with a *zap*.

"Hey!" Ginny hollered. "Why'd you do that? Turn it back on!" She was already on her feet, racing to the TV, but Kansas stopped her and pinned her arms to her sides.

"You're not allowed to watch that movie," he told her. "It's stupid."

"I am *too* allowed to watch it! Let me go!"

Kansas would not let go. Even as Ginny wiggled in his arms, he held her still and tried to talk sense to her.

213

"You just want to watch it 'cause you want that to happen to Mom and Dad," he said. "You want them to get back together."

"Yeah, so?" Ginny reached out a hand to turn the TV back on, but Kansas caught her in time.

"So," he said, "it's not gonna happen."

Five days. It had been five days since Kansas's father had driven back to Oregon. Five days since "talk to you soon!" And not a word since then. Ginny had tried to call him, of course, several times. But she never got ahold of him.

It was time to tell Ginny the truth.

"Dad's never coming back for good," he told her.

"He is too!" Ginny screeched at him. She bit him on the arm then, hard, and when he hollered and let her go, she raced into the hallway. Kansas chased after her, but she got to their bedroom first and slammed the door. "You don't know what you're talking about, Kansas!" she shouted from the other side. Kansas tried to force the door open, but Ginny had her whole body against it, and she was stronger than she looked. "You don't even know! He *is*

coming back. He's gonna move here and live with us. You'll see."

Kansas gave up and slumped to the ground, his back against the door.

"He loves us," Ginny said from the other side.

"Ginny." Kansas tried to make his voice steady. Calm. "Mom and Dad are getting a divorce."

"They are *not*! Dad's gonna move here. He *is*."

Kansas sighed. "He left before," he told Ginny. Kansas didn't want to tell her, he hadn't ever wanted to tell her, but he needed to. It was the only way she would understand. "You don't remember because you were too little, but he left before. He went away all of a sudden, just like this time. And it would have been better if he'd never come back at all."

Even through the thickness of the door, Kansas could make out the unmistakable sound of Ginny sniffling. She was quiet for a moment, then, "I don't believe you."

Kansas plucked a piece of lint out of the carpet. "It's true," he said. "You were three. And he left for a month."

Another sniffle. Kansas could just picture her, wiping her nose with her sleeve. "But he came back," she said softly. "He came back, and that means he loves us. And he'll come back again."

About a foot away, Kansas spied another piece of lint and leaned over to yank it out of the carpet, rolling it between his fingers into a tiny ball. "He came back," he said, choosing each word carefully, "because you got sick."

"I got sick?" Ginny asked. *Sniffle.*

"Yeah. It was when . . . It was the first time we figured out you were allergic to peanuts, and you had to go to the hospital, and everyone was really worried about you, and you were hooked up to all these machines and we thought you might . . ." Kansas could still remember Ginny's little three-year-old face, blotchy and red and scared as they raced her to the hospital. "It was awful," he told her. "And that's why Dad came back."

Sniffle. When Ginny spoke again, her voice was a whimper. "But he came back," she said. "And he stayed. And he loved us."

Kansas sighed again. He didn't know how to explain it. When his father had come back that time, Kansas had been just like Ginny—six years old and *so excited* to see his father. But somehow, all along, in the back of his mind, he'd known. He'd known that his dad was going to leave again. That it was just a matter of time before he left for good. Did he love them? Kansas didn't know. He thought maybe he did, in some way, but not in the way that made you stick around and be a dad.

Not enough.

Kansas dropped the lint back on the carpet and stood up slowly. He took a deep breath. He wanted, more than anything, for Ginny to understand, so he told her clearly and carefully.

"Mom and Dad are never getting back together," he said for the last time. "Not ever. So you should stop hoping."

Even as he walked away, Kansas could hear Ginny's sobs.

23.

A granola bar

Samson woke Francine up three times Saturday night, *wheek*ing from inside his cage, begging to play. Francine figured he was probably restless because he'd been left alone, bored for the past two days while she was at her dad's house, so when he woke her up the third time, she finally gave in. "You need attention, Squeaky Squeaks?" she asked, padding across the carpet to his cage.

At eight thirty, Francine's mother pushed open the door to find Francine guiding Samson through a new guinea pig obstacle course made out of a pair of pajama pants. Samson was supposed to go in one leg, then out the other. But he kept getting confused in the waist area.

"He's not the brightest bulb, is he?" Francine's mother said from the doorway, watching Samson turn in circles inside a pant leg. "Although he sure is adorable."

Francine smiled, rescuing Samson from the pants and cradling him to her chest. He needed a lot of work before they starred in their TV show together. Francine needed a lot of work too. She hated to admit it, but she'd been absolutely freaked out in front of the camera on Friday, and not only because of the booger and the barfing. Being on the other end of that blinking green light had turned out to be a lot more nerve-racking than she'd expected.

"You better get dressed if we're going to make yoga," her mother continued. "Breakfast is already on the table. Oh, and Francine?" her mother said, turning around in the doorway. "Your father and I finally figured out Christmas plans this year."

Francine didn't realize how hard she must've been squeezing Samson until—

Squeak!

"Uh, Christmas?" Francine said, loosening her grip.

"Yes. You'll be here Christmas Eve and early the

morning after. And then your father will take you to church, and you'll have Christmas dinner with him. Your father said he'd get a Christmas tree too, so you'll have two to decorate this year. Won't that be nice?"

Squeak!

Francine must have been super-squeezing Samson again, because he shot out of her hands and across the floor. And by the time Francine had scooped him up and shut him safely back in his cage, her mother had already left the room. She hadn't even waited for an answer to her question.

All through yoga class, Francine tried to twist her body the way Lulu showed them, but she found that what was really twisted was her mind.

Christmas morning with her mom and Christmas evening with her dad—splitting the day right in two. How was her father going to wake her up with a steaming mug of eggnog? How was she supposed to hear her mother singing all her favorite Christmas hymns in church, in her beautiful, clear voice? Was this the way it was going to be every single year from now on?

Francine was so busy thinking about the mess her parents had gotten her into with their stupid divorce that it took her a while to notice that Ginny was in an even more sour mood than she was. She wasn't giggly and tumbly, the way she'd been the week before. In fact, she looked downright depressed.

"You okay?" Francine whispered to her when they were lying on their backs next to each other on their yoga mats, feet up in the air, in the "double leg raise" position.

Ginny frowned. "I'm trying to think of a good trick," she whispered back.

Francine scrunched up her eyebrows.

"Like in *The Parent Trap*," Ginny explained. "A trick to get my dad to come back. I bet the twins in that movie would come up with something real good. I just need to think."

"Girls?" Lulu called from the front. "Let's focus on our breathing, okay?"

It wasn't until class was over and Francine was out in the hallway chomping on her granola bar that she realized what she should have told Ginny—that when it came to figuring out the right thing to do to solve problems, Francine was

221

the absolute wrong person to ask. She never knew exactly what to say, or exactly what to do. Maybe the person Ginny should really be asking for help was that great older brother of hers.

But . . . where *was* Ginny? She wasn't in the bathroom, because Francine had just come from there. And she wasn't by the front door with the parents. No, there was Mrs. Muñoz, with her coat on, waiting for her. So where could she . . .

That's when Francine spotted it—a figure in the now-empty yoga room. She could see it through the glass wall. Ginny. Lying on the floor. At first Francine thought she was practicing her yoga cool-down, the one Lulu had taught them just that morning. But she wasn't. Because her eyes were closed, and she was shaking.

And she was holding an open granola bar.

"Ginny!" Francine screamed.

Everything was a blur after that. Really, Francine didn't remember much at all. But what they told her—her mother and Lulu, after it was over—was that Francine had raced like a freight train to get the grown-ups' attention. And they told her that Mrs. Muñoz had jabbed something into

Ginny's leg, some sort of medicine she carried in her purse. And then they told her that while Mrs. Muñoz was giving Ginny the medicine, Francine—all on her own, without waiting for anyone—had dug through her mother's yoga bag and found her cell phone and dialed 911. That's what they told her.

What Francine really remembered was afterward, when the paramedics had loaded Ginny into the ambulance and the sirens had faded off into the distance, wailing their way to the hospital. That's when Francine began to cry, right on the floor of the yoga room, her shoulders heaving in giant sobs.

Her mother came and sat beside her, folding her legs to squeeze right up next to her. "Shhh," she said, cradling Francine into her arms and patting her head. "It's okay, sweetie. It's all going to be okay." She rocked her softly as she spoke, and Francine let the words melt over her, like butter on toast. "They said she'd be just fine, Francine. The paramedics said she'd be okay. You did exactly the right thing. You knew exactly what to do."

24. A BOUQUET OF FLOWERS

Kansas was sitting in the padded chair next to Ginny's hospital bed when she finally woke up. He wasn't sure at first if she *had* actually woken up, because it was hard to tell if a person was awake if you weren't looking at them, and Kansas definitely didn't want to look at Ginny. She seemed so tiny huddled up under that blue blanket, her face red and patchy and those cords sunk into her arm. He'd pretty much rather look at anything else.

"Kansas?"

He finally lifted his head.

"You're awake," he said. He tried to smile, but it was hard. She'd fallen asleep a while ago, about four hours after they got to the hospital, and the doctors said she was perfectly fine, all better, that she just needed to rest, but it wasn't until Kansas saw her open her eyes again that he realized he'd spent all that time holding his breath, waiting.

"Where's Mom?" Ginny asked.

"Getting coffee. She'll be back in a sec. Or"—Kansas set his video game on the ground—"I could go get her. Want me to get her?"

Ginny shook her head. "S'okay."

Kansas leaned back in his chair. "You feel all right?" Ginny gave him a lying-down shrug. "I could get you water or something."

"No, thanks."

"Oh. Okay. Well, tell me if you want some later."

"Hey, Kansas?" Ginny asked. "When's Dad gonna be here?"

Kansas turned his video game on, then immediately off again. "What?"

"Dad." She was looking at Kansas like he was a moron. "When's he gonna be here?"

And all of a sudden, Kansas understood. He understood, and he wished he didn't. "Ginny," he said, in his softest, most older-brother voice, "Dad's not coming."

Ginny frowned, and five deep wrinkles appeared on her forehead. "Didn't Mom call him?" she asked.

Kansas nodded. "Yeah," he said. "She called him." Kansas had been sitting right in that chair when their mom had called from her cell phone. She'd gone in the hallway so Kansas wouldn't hear the conversation, but he heard it anyway. It was a lot of "but you *need* to be here" and "your business can wait!" and "she's your *daughter,* for Christ's sake, Nick." And when she'd finally come back in the room, she'd just looked at Kansas, her lips tight together, and shook her head slowly.

"But . . . ," Ginny started. But she didn't finish her sentence. Even Kansas knew there was nothing that came after that "but."

"That's why you did it, huh?" Kansas asked.

"What?" Ginny said.

"The granola bar. That's why you took a bite. So Dad would come back, like last time."

Ginny scrunched her knees up under the covers, two

blue lumps, and hugged them close to her chest. But she didn't say anything, just began to sniffle.

Kansas set his video game on the floor again and crawled into the bed next to Ginny, on top of the covers. He snuggled in close, resting her tiny rat's nest of a head on top of his shoulder.

"That was pretty stupid, you know," he told her, patting down her hair.

Ginny sniffled.

"You're pretty much the world's biggest moron." He smoothed her hair as best he could, and Ginny snuggled back into him and closed her eyes.

"Hey, Kansas?"

"Yeah?"

"He's never gonna come back for real, is he?"

"No," he told her. "I don't think he is."

Ginny wiped her nose. "Good," she said.

Kansas pulled away to look at her.

"We don't need him," she said. "Do we, Kansas? We don't need anybody."

"Yeah," Kansas replied. He went back to petting her hair. "We're going to be just fine."

They were still sitting like that, snuggled in close, when Ginny suddenly bolted up in bed and shouted, "Hey, she came!"

"What?" Kansas asked. He followed Ginny's gaze to the hallway, but he didn't see anything. "Who came? What are you talking about?"

"Franny," Ginny said. "My friend from yoga class. I saw her hair, just now in the hallway."

"Franny?"

"Yeah. You know her, from the announcements. She's the girl who saved my life."

Ginny was talking gibberish. Kansas was just standing up, to go find their mom or a nurse or anyone, when he saw her. Stepping into the room, holding a bouquet of flowers, her green hair as bright as a traffic light.

"*Francine?*"

"*Kansas?*"

Ginny clapped her hands together. "Oh, good!" she said. "You're friends already!"

Francine dropped her flowers on the floor.

228

25.

A unicycle

It wasn't like Francine became insta-friends with Kansas or anything. Being able to stand someone was not the same as liking them. But the fact was that Francine *was* able to stand Kansas after that. Partly it was because she knew that Ginny was his little sister, and it was hard to hate someone with a sister that cute. But it was also because they shared something—even if Kansas didn't know they shared it. His parents were getting a divorce, just like Francine's were. Somehow that one little fact changed everything.

The weirdest thing, though, was that suddenly it seemed like Kansas was able to stand her too. Because before school on Monday morning, when Francine saw Kansas in front of the main steps, and she shuffled her feet and said, "Hey, um, good morning," he didn't ignore her or shout at her or do any of the things she thought he might. He just said, "Yeah. I mean, hi." And then at lunch, when Luis insisted they have an emergency meeting of the Media Club, Francine managed to sit right across the table from Kansas without even rolling her eyes once. It took a lot of effort, but she didn't. She thought for a second that Kansas maybe even sort of grinned at her. But he might have just had to burp.

"All right," Luis said, his elbows bent at sharp angles on the lunch table. "We need a plan."

Natalie peeled the aluminum foil off a chocolate pudding cup and slid it across the table to Alicia, along with a plastic spoon. Francine ignored them as she dug into her leftover spinach-wrapped flounder with lentils, smiling like mushy fish was her favorite food in the world. "A plan for what?" she asked.

"To buy a new camera," Luis told them. "Media Club is canceled until we get one, right? And Miss Sparks says the club doesn't have any funds. So we need to figure out how to raise the money ourselves. I did research, and the cheapest one that will work costs a hundred and seventy-nine dollars."

"A hundred and seventy-nine dollars? How are we supposed to get *that*?" Emma said. "It sure is a cucumber."

"Huh?" Francine asked.

"You mean a pickle," Alicia said to Emma. "It sure is a *pickle*."

"Yeah," Emma replied. "A pickle."

It had been strange not meeting for Media Club that morning. Francine had arrived at school at 8:05, just like everyone else. She'd walked through the crowded hallways, just like everyone else, and she'd sat down in her regular seat, just like everyone else. And just like everyone else, she'd listened to Mrs. Weinmore drone out the announcements over the intercom. Francine had missed sitting behind that camera more than she'd thought she would.

"What about a bake sale?" she asked. "Or a car wash?"

Natalie shook her head. "Nah," she said. "My sisters are always having to do bake sales and car washes for cheerleading, and it's tons of work, and they barely even make any money."

"Oh." Francine's face dropped.

Brendan crushed his empty soda can with his fist, then

tossed it over all their heads, toward the trash can at the far end. It bounced off the rim of the trash can and across the cafeteria floor. "I think Francine and Kansas should have to pay for the camera," he said, not moving a muscle to pick up his can. "They were the ones who did the dares, and it was a dare that made the camera break."

"Yeah," Andre agreed. "Francine and Kansas should pay for it."

"No way!" Francine said. "I don't have a hundred and seventy-nine dollars."

"Me, neither," Kansas replied. "I don't even have a hundred and seventy-nine cents."

"Anyway, *Brendan*," Alicia sneered, "it's not their fault it broke. Emma was the one who barfed on it."

"Hey!" Emma cried. "I couldn't help it. I got sick. And anyway," she said to Alicia, "if *you* hadn't gone to the dentist, then none of this would've happened in the first place."

Natalie reached across the table and patted Emma's arm. Alicia's, too. "It's neither of you guys' fault," she said. "If it's anyone's fault, it's Brendan's. It was his dares that got everyone barfing. And he gave them those dares without even letting us vote on them first."

"Yeah," Emma said. "We were supposed to vote. You totally cheated, Brendan."

"You're just mad because you broke the camera," Brendan shot back.

"Did not!"

"Did too!"

And just like that they were grumbling and growling, every single one of them, pointing fingers at each other and being, Francine felt, utterly unproductive.

"Look," she finally cut in, "it's no one's fault. We all just have to work together to fix it. *Right?*" Everyone reluctantly mumbled in agreement. "We need to think of something really good, that's all. Some way that can definitely earn money."

They all became silent, thinking.

Suddenly, Luis slapped a hand on the table. "I've got it!" he said. "The talent show!"

Francine's head snapped up. "What?"

"The prize," Luis said. "For winning the talent show. It's two hundred dollars."

Emma clapped her hands together. "That would be enough to buy a new camera!"

F.H.

"Yeah," Francine said slowly. "It would. But only if we win. Some of the kids who compete are *amazing*."

"That's true," Natalie said with a frown. "Remember last year, that kid who played the piano with his feet?"

"Oh, my gosh," Emma put in, "or Tanya and Teresa's gymnastics act? They did, like, ten one-handed cartwheels in a row."

"Yeah," Francine agreed. "And ours would have to be better."

"Well, one of us has to be able to do *something*," Alicia said. "Can anyone here do anything really cool? Like juggle fire or ride a unicycle? Mr. Paulsen has a unicycle in the drama room, I've seen it. Someone could ride that, all around the stage."

Around the table, there were slow shakes of heads. No one, it seemed, knew how to do anything cool. They were all quiet again, until . . .

"Francine and Kansas should do it."

It was Brendan who said it. Francine snapped her head in his direction, and she saw it—that mischievous smile of his that was becoming all too familiar.

"What?" she cried.

"Huh?" Kansas spurted.

"It's perfect," Brendan said as the other members of the Media Club turned his way. "I mean, right now you two are tied, right? Eight to eight. Because Kansas didn't finish the last dare?" Kansas grumbled into the neck of his sweatshirt, but Brendan kept right on talking. "So, we should have one move dare. As, like, a tie-breaker. Whoever wins the talent show wins the war and gets to be the news anchor. What do you think?"

All around the table, the members of the Media Club nodded.

"Sounds fair to me," Alicia said.

"Good idea, Brendan," Emma agreed.

"I think it sounds *brilliant,*" Andre put in.

"Let's make it official," Luis said. "All in favor?"

Everybody except Kansas and Francine raised their hands. The dare was officially on.

On the way home from school, Francine convinced her dad to swing by her mom's house to pick up Samson. That guinea pig, Francine realized, was her ticket to winning the talent show on Friday. What judge *wouldn't* vote for an adorable furry creature with big sappy brown eyes? Especially if he could do lots of great tricks, like leap over walls and crawl through mazelike tubes.

Only . . . Samson hadn't quite seemed to figure out that was what he needed to be doing.

"Aw, come *on,* Samson!" she cried when Samson got lost in his tunnel for the fourth time. He'd been in there for five minutes, snuffling and snorting and generally doing everything but coming out the other end. "We're never going to win if you keep that up." So far the only thing Samson had done correctly every single time was walk in a straight line to get a guinea pig treat. And no judge was going to give her two hundred dollars for *that.*

Francine stuffed her hand into the tube and coaxed Samson out. He snuggled his warm body against her palms, cute as ever, with his tufts of fur peeking out between her fingers. But Francine was still mad at him.

"Maybe he's just nervous," Francine's father piped up. He was sitting on the couch, drawing in his sketchbook.

He'd been working on a new machine—Francine had taken a peek in the car. This one would be thirty steps long, and end with a carton of milk tipping over into an empty glass. "It's a lot of pressure on the little guy," he said, "trying to win a talent show. Maybe Samson just has stage fright. Some of us were never meant to be in the spotlight."

Francine's father grinned at her, like he thought he was being funny. But Francine didn't grin back. She was still mad at him too.

After dinner—pizza from Carlino's, again—Francine walked across the street to Kansas's house. Mainly, she wanted to see how Ginny was doing. Partially, she also wanted to try to wiggle some information out of Kansas and find out what he was planning to do for the talent show.

When she rang the doorbell, a woman answered who must've been Kansas's mom.

"Um, hi," Francine said. "I'm Francine, and—"

But she wasn't able to finish her sentence, because Kansas's mother immediately wrapped her up in a bear hug.

"Thank you, Francine," she said when she'd finally let go. "For everything. I was so sorry I missed you at the hospital. I really wanted to meet you. Thank you for being such a good friend. To both Ginny and Kansas."

"Uh, yeah," Francine said. "No problem. I—" But Kansas's mother was back to hugging her again.

After what felt like a century, Kansas's mom finally stopped hugging Francine and led her through the house, past a beat-up corduroy couch and a tiny Christmas tree bursting with ornaments. "Ginny's resting right now," she told Francine as they walked. "But I'm sure she'll be thrilled to see you."

"Franny!" Ginny shouted the second she laid eyes on Francine. She was in bed, tucked beneath her covers, but she looked a million times sunnier than she had the day before. Scraps of green construction paper were strewn across her bed, and she was wielding a pair of scissors, which Francine carefully avoided as she bustled across the room for a hug. "Your hair is starting to fade," Ginny told Francine, squeezing her in tight.

"Really?" Francine plucked a strand of green hair away from her face and examined it. "Huh. Maybe it is."

"You gonna dye it back?" Ginny said. "I really like it green."

Francine laughed.

From the doorway, Kansas's mom told them, "I'll let you two catch up. But just fifteen minutes, okay? Ginny needs her rest."

"Aw, *Mom.*"

"Ginny, I don't want you to overdo it. Be calm, you hear me?"

"Mo-*om.*"

"*Calm.*" She shut the door.

Francine peered around the room. There was a small pile of unpacked boxes in the corner, and posters all over the walls. And there was a second bed against the far wall, and a thick line of masking tape separating the two sides.

"You share with Kansas?" Francine asked.

"Yep. There used to be a wall of boxes in the middle, but Kansas took it down. Now it's just the tape. He loves sharing with me. We're like best friends."

"He's not home?"

"Nah," Ginny replied. "He's next door practicing for the talent show."

"Oh?" Francine sat down gingerly on the edge of the bed, careful not to smush Ginny's construction paper scraps. "Do you, um, know what his act is?"

"He's gonna ride a unicycle," Ginny said, picking up a piece of green paper and aiming her scissors at it. "I think he borrowed it from one of the teachers at school. Won't that be great?"

Francine frowned. Riding a unicycle was *way* better than having a guinea pig who could only walk in a straight line. "Yeah," she agreed. "Great."

"You wanna help me make a Christmas tree?" Ginny asked her. She passed Francine one of her scraps of green paper. "I wanna make it as tall as the ceiling, but I'm not good at cutting."

Francine took the paper, and the scissors too. "Sure," she said. "Why not?"

While Francine cut, Ginny directed her, chattering about Christmas trees and ornaments and all the presents she was going to ask Santa for. And mostly Francine listened. Mostly. But she also thought.

She thought about Kansas riding a unicycle, and how he was probably going to win the talent show. And she thought about how, as soon as he *did* win, everything that Francine had worked so hard for—becoming the news anchor, beating Kansas in the dare war—was going to be all for nothing. And then she thought about how, in the end, maybe that wasn't as terrible as she'd thought it would be.

Not that Francine *wanted* Kansas to win the dare war. Not that she *wanted* to lose the news anchor job. But at least if Kansas won the talent show, he'd be able to save the Media Club. And maybe saving the club was more important than beating Kansas Bloom. If she could just get back behind a camera, she thought, she'd be pretty happy. Even if it *was* aimed at Kansas.

After Ginny's mom came in and told them that it was time for Francine to go home, Francine hugged Ginny good-bye and let herself out the front door. And it was then that she heard the terrible crash from next door.

Screeeeeeeeeeeech! THUD.

Francine poked her head over the fence to the neighbor's driveway, and that's how she found Kansas—facedown on the concrete beneath a unicycle, his legs splayed at odd angles.

"Are you okay?" she asked, bustling next door to help him up.

Kansas was back on his feet before she got there. "I'm fine," he grumbled, dusting off the knees of his jeans. "I was just trying a new trick." He yanked the unicycle up by the seat. "My act's really good. I'm totally going to beat you." But Francine could tell, by the way he avoided her gaze as he spoke, that Kansas was lying. His act was just as rotten as hers was.

"Oh," Francine said. "Good. Mine's really great too."

"Great," Kansas replied. "It'll be a really good show then."

"Yeah. Well . . ." Francine shuffled her feet. It was hard to believe that the Media Club was going to be over for good. Just like that. "Um, well, anyway, I guess I should go." She gestured vaguely across the street. "I just came to check on Ginny. She's, um, she seems better today. I was helping her make a Christmas tree."

Kansas shook his head. "Is she still doing that?"

"Yep. She says she wants to tape it to the wall and glue you guys' ornaments on it. I tried to tell her they'd probably fall off, but—"

"That's what I said too!" Kansas cried. Their eyes met briefly, and then Kansas shot his back down to the ground again. "I *told* her we already have a tree, but she says the one Mom got this year isn't big enough." He snorted. "Whoever heard of having two Christmas trees?"

Francine laughed. "I have two Christmas trees," she told him.

"Really?"

"Yeah. One at my mom's and one at my dad's. 'Cause my parents are getting a divorce and—"

Francine stopped talking. Her heart skipped a beat. The words had just tumbled out of her mouth. *My parents are getting a divorce.* She'd really said it. Out loud. "My parents are getting a divorce," she said again, just to hear how it sounded.

Kansas kept his eyes on his feet. "I, um, already knew," he told her.

"You did? How?"

"I read a note you got from the office. I was going to tell you that day you IM'd me, but then you—"

"What are you talking about?" Francine asked. Maybe he'd fallen over one too many times that afternoon. "I never IM'd you. I'm not even allowed to use IM."

"Sure you did. When you dared me to wear Ginny's tutu. You were super mean. That's why I dared you to dye your hair."

Yep, Kansas had definitely lost it. "I never dared you to do that," Francine told him.

Kansas froze, his mouth open. He wrenched it closed, then opened it again, slowly. "Really?" he said.

"Really."

"You *swear?*"

Francine nodded, and Kansas cocked his head to the side. "Who do you think it was, then?"

Francine shrugged. "No idea."

"Francine!" There was a call from across the street. Her dad. Francine could see him in the parking lot of their apartment complex.

"Yeah?" Francine shouted back, cupping her hands to her mouth. "What is it?"

"Time to come in, pea pod! It's getting late."

For the first time, Francine realized that the sky was dimming—had dimmed. It was dark, murky. She could even make out several stars in the sky.

244

"Be there in a sec!" she hollered. Her father nodded and hiked back up the stairs to the apartment.

She turned to Kansas. "Look," she said, before she could stop the words she knew she needed to say. "I know you said your talent show act was really good, but . . ." Kansas rolled his unicycle slowly back and forth across the driveway, avoiding her gaze. "Well, one of us needs to win, to save the club. And I was thinking"—Francine took a deep breath—"would you maybe want to work together?"

Kansas stopped rolling the unicycle. "Why would you want to work with me?" he said.

"To save the club. I just *told* you."

"Is this some sort of trick?" Kansas asked.

"No, it's—"

"Francine!" It was her father again, leaning his head out the window. *"Pea pod!"*

"Coming!" She turned back to Kansas. "Just forget it," she said. "I'll do it by myself." Maybe there was still time to train Samson. "I thought maybe you actually cared about the club, but I guess not."

"I care," Kansas said.

Francine rolled her eyes. "You hated the club from the very first day. You never even wanted to be in it."

Kansas pressed his thumb hard into the unicycle seat. "Not everyone can be the star of the club like you, Francine," he said.

Francine raised an eyebrow. What was he talking about? Francine wasn't the star of the club. If anyone was the star, it was Alicia. She was the news anchor.

"I want to save the club too, you know," he told her. "But what am I supposed to do? I can't even ride a stupid unicycle. You want me to just get up on stage and pour a glass of milk or something? Who would pay two hundred dollars for *that*?"

Francine blinked.

"What?" Kansas said. "Why are you looking at me like that? Do I have something in my teeth?"

Suddenly Francine's heart felt a million times lighter, as though all her worries had been lifted away. "I've got it," she said, allowing a smile to stretch across her face. "I know what we're going to do in the talent show."

26. A HAMMER

Of all the tools in Mr. Muñoz's workshop—the drill, the buzz saw, the grinder—it turned out that the one Kansas liked the best was the hammer. There was something calming about pounding a nail into a piece of wood, feeling the wood give at the very last minute when the nail finally went through.

"Looking good, Kansas," Mr. Muñoz told him, stepping back into the garage holding two cans of soda. "Coke or Dr Pepper?"

Kansas's mom never let him have caffeine at night. "Dr Pepper, please," he said, setting down the hammer. Mr. Muñoz tossed him the can. Kansas caught it, then tapped on the top with his fingernail a few times before popping back the lid. It opened with a satisfying *fizz,* and Kansas took a good long gulp.

"Why do you tap it?" Mr. Muñoz asked him when Kansas had set his can on the workbench beside him. "Before you open it?"

Kansas readjusted his plastic goggles. "It, like, settles the soda." He picked up his hammer again, then set a nail against the large piece of plywood, right where Mr. Muñoz had marked it. "The carbonation or whatever. So it won't spray out when you open it." Now that Kansas thought about it, he wasn't sure any of that was true at all. But Will had always done it, so Kansas had too, for as long as he could remember.

"Huh," Mr. Muñoz said. He tapped a few times on the top of his Coke, then popped the top—no foam. "Well, how 'bout that?"

Kansas and Francine had been coming over to Mr. Muñoz's workshop every afternoon that week to work on their talent show act. It was a ton of work, and there was no way they could have done it without Mr. Muñoz. Kansas could hardly believe they'd done it at all. It had been three days of measuring, sawing, and nailing, long into the evening, and somehow they were almost completely done. Francine was at her mom's tonight, so it was up to Kansas to work on the finishing touches.

"So tell me again," Mr. Muñoz said, strapping on a pair of goggles to match Kansas's. He picked up a second hammer. "If you guys win the talent show tomorrow night, then you get to read the morning announcements for the rest of the year together? Is that the deal?"

"Sort of," Kansas told him. "If we win, me and Francine will be tied, nine to nine. But . . ." Kansas hadn't told anyone yet about what he'd been thinking the past few days, but he supposed it couldn't hurt to tell Mr. Muñoz. "I think if we win, I'm going to let Francine be news anchor by herself."

"Don't *you* want to be news anchor?" Mr. Muñoz asked.

Kansas shrugged. He hadn't wanted it at first, not at all. But sitting behind that desk last Friday had actually been sort of fun—the heat of the lights, the rush of the moment—much more fun than he'd expected. Well, before the barfing and getting suspended part, obviously. But Francine, she'd wanted it all along. So badly. It had been her idea about the talent show too. And she really was the hardest-working member of the club. So Kansas couldn't help thinking that maybe she deserved it a little more.

"Well, whatever happens," Mr. Muñoz said, "I'll be there tomorrow night, front and center. Ramona and I already bought our tickets."

Kansas squinted at the old man through his goggles. "You're coming? To the talent show?"

"Of course! You think I'd miss the world's most amazing talent show act?"

"Oh," Kansas said. He was concentrating so hard on the piece of wood in front of him that it took him a second to notice that Mr. Muñoz had put down his hammer. "What?" Kansas asked. The old man was looking at him curiously. "Did I mess up? What did I do?"

"No, nothing like that," Mr. Muñoz said. "I just wanted to be sure that . . . I thought I might have upset you, that's all. I shouldn't have invited myself to your talent show. But I would really like to be there, Kansas, if that's okay with you."

Kansas picked up his Dr Pepper and took a long, fizzy gulp. Then another. "You can come, I guess," he said, "if you really want to." It was a free country, wasn't it? Kansas set his soda back down on the workbench. "But, I mean, if something else comes up and you can't come, I won't be mad or anything."

Mr. Muñoz waited until Kansas was looking at him again before he said what he did next. "I wouldn't miss it for the world," he told him when their eyes met. "I'll be there. I promise."

And even though Kansas knew that promises were easier to break than toothpicks, for some reason, this time, he believed it. He picked up another nail and began to hammer.

27.

<u>A plastic spoon</u>

There were still three hours before the talent show started, but Francine couldn't stop pacing. She paced on the rug in front of the TV in the living room. What if she and Kansas didn't pull it off? What would she do without Media Club? She paced in front of the couch. What if they *did* pull it off? Who would be the news anchor then? Maybe she could convince Kansas to let her do it all by herself. After all, the whole talent show act *had* been her idea.

Francine had just moved to the kitchen to do more pacing there, when the phone rang. She snatched the cordless off the counter. "Hello?"

"Pea pod! Just the girl I was looking for."

"Oh, hey, Dad. What's up? You're still coming tonight, right?"

"Of course. I just had a thought about Christmas, and I wanted to run it by you real quick."

"Yeah?" Francine picked a lemon out of the bowl on the counter.

"Well, more of an inspiration, really. I get you for Christmas dinner, right? So I was thinking. I'm no good at turkey like your mother, but how would you feel about pizza?"

"Pizza?" Francine rolled the lemon across the counter. Takeout from Carlino's did not sound like Christmas.

"Yeah. You remember Mr. Jules at the college? He has a pizza stone, makes his own dough and everything, and he said he'd teach me a few tricks. I've been looking up recipes. We can do whatever you want—pesto, Parmesan, even just plain old pepperoni if that floats your boat."

"Wait. You mean . . . make the pizza ourselves?" Francine placed the lemon back in the bowl. "But you burn water."

Her dad laughed. "We'll make three pizzas," he said, "in case I wreck the first two."

Francine allowed herself a tiny smile at that. "Can we flip the dough in the air like those guys on TV?"

"We'll make *nine*," her father replied, "so we can drop at least seven. What do you say? I thought it might be nice to start our own little traditions, just us two."

Francine thought about that. Christmas wasn't going to be the same this year, that was for sure. But maybe that wasn't entirely a terrible thing.

"Yeah," she said. "That might be okay."

"Good. I'll see you soon, pea pod."

"Bye, Dad."

When Francine hung up the phone, she saw her mom walking into the kitchen, an empty tea mug in her hands.

"Hey there," she greeted Francine. "You all set for tonight?"

Francine didn't answer, just watched her mom walk to the sink and rinse out her mug. All this time, she realized, she'd been looking for the exact right thing to do to get her parents back together again. And all this time, she'd thought she couldn't because she wasn't smart enough to figure out what the exact right thing was.

But when Ginny had gotten sick—when she'd eaten that

granola bar—Francine had known what to do right away. She hadn't even needed a second to think about it.

Maybe there *wasn't* a solution to fixing Francine's parents, the way there had been with Ginny and the granola bar. Maybe they were going to get a divorce no matter what Francine did.

"Mom?" she said as her mother opened the dishwasher.

"Mm-hmm?"

"Can we go caroling this year? On Christmas Eve? It's just . . ." Her mother set the mug on the top rack and turned to look at her. Francine took a deep breath. "We always say we're gonna go, every year, and we never do. I'm not gonna get to sing with you this year in church and . . ."

Francine's mother crossed the kitchen slowly, then wrapped Francine up in a hug. "Absolutely," she told her, and Francine buried her face in her mother's sweater. It smelled like lavender soap. "That sounds like a perfect idea." She lifted up Francine's face then and inspected her carefully, both hands cupped below her ears. "You are turning into a beautiful young lady, you know that?"

"*Mo*-om."

"Even with the green hair."

255

Francine laughed.

Her mother kissed her on the forehead. "Anything you need for tonight?" she asked.

"Nah. Everything's all ready. Kansas and Mr. Muñoz are driving it to the school in Mr. Muñoz's truck. I said I'd meet them an hour early to set up."

"Sounds good. You want to see if Natalie's around? You two could hang out for a few hours, and then we could all drive over together."

Francine shrugged, which was supposed to mean no, but apparently her mother was not good at reading body language.

"Anything to keep you from pacing," she said, handing Francine the cordless phone off the counter. "Natalie hasn't been over in weeks. It will be nice to see her."

Francine stared at the phone in her hands for a while, then slowly set it down on the counter.

"Sweetie?" her mom said.

"I'm going to get Samson ready for tonight," Francine told her, heading for the kitchen door. When she reached the stairs, she climbed them two at a time.

• • •

Kansas was late.

Francine had been sitting on the props table behind the stage of the school auditorium for fifteen minutes, waiting for him, but he hadn't shown up yet. Francine huffed. This was just like Kansas, she thought. You go and trust him for one second, and then he was *late*.

The backstage area was mostly deserted, just a couple of high school volunteers dressed in black, running around yelling into headsets. Francine looked at the clock on the wall—forty-four minutes until the show officially started. Butterflies were growing in her stomach again, just the way they had been when she co-anchored the news with Kansas. She tried to squelch them, kicking her legs under the table. How would she ever be a TV animal trainer if she had stage fright all the time? Next to her, Samson grunted from his cage.

"You need help?"

Francine looked up. There was Natalie, her backpack slung over one arm.

"What are you doing here?" Francine asked. Which, she

257

realized after the words came out of her mouth, was maybe not the nicest way she could have phrased things.

Natalie shrugged. "Me and Alicia signed up to do refreshments in the lobby," she said. "But I saw your mom, and she said you needed help back here." Natalie looked around, as though noticing for the first time that there was nothing to set up.

"It's not here yet," Francine explained.

"Oh." Natalie hoisted her backpack higher on her shoulder. "Um, I guess I should go back to the refreshments, then."

"Yeah," Francine said. "Or, um." She stuck a pointer finger in Samson's cage and stroked his silky hair. "You could wait with me. If you want."

Natalie glanced over her shoulder, deciding. "Okay," she said at last. She dropped her backpack on the table and climbed up to sit on the other side of Samson. "What're you doing for the talent show anyway?" she asked Francine. "Did you teach Samson some more tricks?"

Francine squinted at her. Natalie might know what her act was if she ever bothered to talk to her anymore. "It's a surprise," she said.

"Oh."

They sat in silence.

Francine checked the clock on the wall again. Forty-two minutes until the talent show.

"Hey, Natalie?" she asked suddenly.

"Yeah?" Natalie was hunched over Samson's cage, petting him through the bars.

"It's just . . ." It had been three weeks since Thanksgiving, and not *once* had Natalie even said so much as, "Hey, Francine, you seem a little down. Anything going on?" Hadn't Natalie noticed that Francine had been upset lately? They'd been best friends since baby daycare. You'd think if you'd been friends with someone that long you'd be able to read her mind a little bit, to know what she was thinking. But maybe Natalie just didn't care to know.

"Nothing," Francine said, shaking her head. "Sorry there's nothing for you to help with. You can go back to refreshments if you want."

Natalie looked up from Samson's cage. "I'm not really helping with refreshments," she said.

"You're not?"

"Well, Alicia is. I just came with her 'cause . . . I wanted to give you this."

Francine watched as Natalie unzipped her backpack and pulled something out. It was a chocolate pudding cup. "I thought you might want it," she told Francine. "For good luck." She had one for herself too. "Oh, and, um . . ." She dug in her backpack again, searching for something else. "Here." She handed Francine a plastic spoon.

A best friend, Francine realized then, wasn't someone who could read your mind. A best friend was someone who remembered the plastic spoon.

"Thanks," Francine said softly. She peeled off the lid of the pudding cup, licking the underside. "Hey, Natalie?"

Natalie was peeling her own cup. "Yeah?"

"I have to tell you something."

And so Francine told Natalie all about her parents' divorce, and her dad's new apartment, and two sets of furniture, and two Christmases, and all of it. And Natalie sat there, listening and sometimes saying "whoa, that *stinks*!" and sometimes just nodding and sometimes offering Francine some extra pudding. And when Francine was all done talking and both of their pudding cups were scraped clean, Natalie said, "How come you didn't tell me before?"

And Francine just shrugged.

"Well, anyway," Natalie said. "It'll be okay, I think. I can help you decorate your new room at your dad's if you want."

"Really?"

"Of course. I'm your best friend."

Francine smiled at that. But there was still one naggy question tugging at the back of her brain. "Did you vote for Kansas?"

"What?"

"When we tied for news anchor. Did you vote for him instead of me? You said you thought he was cute, so I thought maybe—"

"No way!" Natalie said. "Just because he's cute doesn't mean I'd vote for him over you."

And Francine knew—the way you know something about someone you've been best friends with since baby daycare—that Natalie was telling the truth.

"I wonder who did," Francine said. "I got three votes.

That's you, me, and either Emma or Alicia. One of them had to have voted for Kansas."

"I guess," Natalie said, but Francine could tell she wasn't really thinking about it anymore. She was looking at something at the far end of the stage. "What the heck is *that*?" she asked.

Francine followed Natalie's gaze. There was Kansas, twenty-five minutes late, with Mr. Muñoz, and they were pushing an enormous object on wheels, covered by a large brown tarp. It was at least three times as tall as Kansas, and twice as long.

"That," Francine told Natalie as the two of them hopped off the table and crossed the stage to meet Kansas, "is our talent show act."

28. A CARTON OF MILK

Kansas thought he'd be sweating bullets before his and Francine's big act, but as it turned out, he was cool as a cucumber.

Francine, on the other hand, was a nervous wreck.

"What if we mess up?" she said, her hands shaking as she fumbled with the lock on Samson's cage. Inside, Samson squeaked, eager to be let out. "What if I forget what I'm supposed to say? What if everyone laughs at us?" Kansas and Francine were waiting in the wings, watching Carl Schumacher finish up his ventriloquist act on stage. Carl was pretty funny, Kansas thought, but not good enough to win two hundred dollars.

"It'll be *fine*," Kansas told her, reaching over to open Samson's cage for her. "There's still one more act before us, so will you just calm down already?"

Francine nodded as she cradled Samson in her arms, stroking his fur. But her hands were still shaking.

"We'll be *fine*," Kansas told her again. He turned to the stage to watch the ventriloquist act.

"Why did the turtle cross the road?" Carl was asking his dummy, Buddy.

"To get to the Shell station!" Buddy replied.

The curtain closed, and Carl and Buddy scuttled off the stage. "Good luck," Carl muttered to Kansas and Francine as he passed them. "It's *scary* out there."

Francine's hands began to shake even faster.

The talent show's MC, a fifth-grader named Violet Montebank, raced onto the stage to announce the next act. Kansas rocked on his feet. Just one more act to sit through and then he and Francine would be up.

"And now," Violet cried from the stage. Her face was yellow from the spotlight. "Please put your hands together for our next big talent, fourth-grader Brendan King and his stupefying magic act!"

Kansas turned to look at Francine. "Huh?" he said.

"It couldn't be . . . ," she began.

But it was. Just at that moment, Brendan King walked on from the wing across the stage. He was wearing a black cape and a tall magician's cap. He waved at the cheering audience.

"Huh?" Kansas said again.

"Thanks, everyone!" Brendan said to the crowd. "And now please welcome my assistant, Andre!"

"What?" Kansas said as Andre appeared on stage too. He waved as well.

"I don't understand," Francine whispered to him as Brendan and Andre began the magic act. "Why would Brendan dare us to win the talent show if he was going to be in it himself?"

Kansas shook his head. It didn't make any sense at all. Until, suddenly, it did. "Brendan wants to be the news anchor!" he cried, turning to Francine. Behind him, the stage manager gave Kansas a stern *shush*ing. "That day at lunch," he went on, lowering his voice. Francine leaned in close to hear him. "Brendan said, 'Whoever wins the talent show gets to be news anchor,' remember?" Francine nodded.

"And we all agreed on it. He was trying to trick us. He thought we'd go out there and look like morons, and he could pull off some cool magic act and win everything."

Francine shook her head. "It was him all along," she said, "tricking us. You know it was his idea to give you that underwear dare? He stole those underwear from you in PE."

Kansas squinted an eye at her. "Those weren't mine," he told her. "He probably just took a pair of his own underwear and wrote my name on them." Francine slapped her forehead. "He's probably the one who IM'd me too, I bet, about wearing Ginny's tutu. I can't *believe* that all this time we never even . . ."

Francine let out a huge sigh. "We might as well give up now," she said, snuggling Samson to her chest. "He's probably been working on this act forever. We'll never win."

"Yeah," Kansas agreed. They were *sunk*.

"Hey, guys?" Kansas felt a tap on his shoulder. It was the stage manager, his hand over his headset. "Have you guys been *watching* this magic act?" he asked them. Kansas and Francine shook their heads. "It is seriously terrible. Look."

So Kansas and Francine watched.

On stage, Andre was holding Brendan's magician's hat brim up. *"Abracadabra!"* Brendan shouted, waving his wand toward the hat. "Assistant, please hand me the rabbit."

Kansas was pretty sure that was the part where Andre was supposed to produce a rabbit out of the hat, but that's not what Andre did. Instead, he tilted the hat to look inside it. "I can't find it," he told Brendan.

The audience let out a tittering of giggles, which Brendan did not seem too pleased about. "Assistant, *please,*" he ordered. "The rabbit."

"It's not in here," Andre told him. "I found your trick thumb, though, you want that?" The audience roared.

By the time Brendan's magic act ended, there was no doubt in Kansas's mind that it was the worst performance he'd ever seen in his life. Even Francine looked relieved. There was no way that Brendan would win the talent show.

On the other hand, Kansas thought, as the main curtains closed and the stage manager helped them wheel their act on stage, it meant that he and Francine were now the only hope that the Media Club had.

"And now," Violet Montebank announced on the other side of the curtain. Behind it, Kansas and Francine raced to make last-minute adjustments to their contraption. Everything had to be *just so,* or it wouldn't work. "For something a little more . . . *unusual.* Please give a round of applause to Francine Halata and Kansas Bloom!"

The audience applauded, and the curtain opened. Kansas could feel the lights on his face, bright and warm. It was kind of a nice feeling.

"Hello," Kansas said to the audience. He made his voice loud and clear, so that everyone could hear him. It was hard to make out faces in the audience, but he could see the judges clearly enough—five of them, sitting in the front row. There were two teachers, two fifth-graders he'd never met, and . . . Mrs. Weinmore. Kansas gulped.

"Um, anyway," he went on, "I bet you're wondering what we're doing with all this." Kansas pointed behind him, at the giant machine he and Francine and Mr. Muñoz had spent the whole week creating. If you didn't know what it was, it would just look like a mess of strange objects and ramps and pulleys, nailed to an enormous wooden structure on wheels. But it was quite a bit more than that. Kansas turned to Francine, waiting for her to do her part of the talking.

But Francine was frozen, still as a statue, except for her shaking hands. She was staring into the spotlight. And she wasn't saying a word.

"Um, Francine?" he whispered, tugging on her sleeve. "It's your turn."

Francine finally snapped to her senses. "Hey, Kansas," she said, going over the lines that they'd rehearsed. Her hands were still shaky, but Kansas could tell she was doing her best not to sound nervous. "I sure feel like some milk." She showed the audience the cup she was holding, a large clear plastic one. "But the milk carton is way up there." She pointed, all the way to the top corner of the wooden structure, where a single carton of milk sat by itself on a wooden platform. "I can't reach it. Can you get it for me?"

"Sure I can," Kansas said. He turned to the audience. "Are you ready?" The audience murmured and nodded. Kansas wasn't sure, but he thought he could see his mother and Ginny in the audience, next to the Muñozes. When

Ginny waved, he knew it was them. "I *said*," he repeated, "are you *READY*?"

At that, the audience let out a resounding *"Yes!"*

Kansas took two objects out of his pocket—a pair of boys' underwear, and a pink pencil with a cherry eraser. "Well, then," he told the audience, "I guess it's time to get Francine some milk." And, just as they had practiced, Kansas stuck the eraser end of the pencil inside the briefs and used them like a slingshot to shoot the pencil *up up up* into the wooden structure.

It was a good thing Kansas had spent so much time playing basketball. His aim was perfect. The pencil hit its mark exactly, *zing*ing right into the broken camera from Media Club.

The camera was screwed into the wooden structure with a hinge, and when the pencil hit the camera, it tilted downward, just enough to knock into a small piece of wood.

The piece of wood had been fashioned into a boat—with a fuzzy photograph for a sail, attached by a mast made of a permanent marker. And when the camera knocked into it, the boat fell off its perch and landed—*plop!*—in a plastic tub filled with water.

The boat floated across the tub, and when it got to the very end, it smashed sail-first into a second pair of underwear, this one hanging from the wall by a hook.

A crumpled ball of pink paper dropped out of the underwear and fell about a foot and a half, where it landed—*kerplop!*—on the head of Francine's guinea pig.

Down on the stage, Kansas could hear Francine sucking in her breath, waiting for Samson to pull off his part of the act. But he did it perfectly, just as he had in rehearsal. As soon as the paper ball landed on him, Samson climbed *up up up* a tiny ladder to a bowl of guinea pig treats, where he began to eat.

The bowl of guinea pig treats was sitting next to Kansas's basketball on a tilty platform, and when Samson ate, the platform shifted, pitching the basketball down a curvy ramp. It rolled around and around and around, until it knocked into . . .

. . . a bottle of green hair dye, which fell off its perch, parachuting down with the help of the sparkly white tutu it was attached to.

The bottle of dye knocked into a CD case that was standing up on its end. That CD knocked into another one, and that knocked into another, and down they all went like dominoes, until the last one crashed into three colored golf balls.

Each of the balls cascaded down a small track, zooming this way and that, at last landing—*plop! plop! plop!*—in an enormous pile of ketchup packets.

The balls landed with such force that one of the ketchup packets flew up and landed—*plonk!*—in an open jar of mustard.

The jar of mustard was attached to a pulley. And when the ketchup flew in, the jar yanked down on its string . . .

. . . and yanked up on the bag of jumbo marshmallows on the other end. Those marshmallows had been sitting on top of one of the legs of a blue swively chair, and when their weight was lifted, the chair began to roll down a slight incline to knock against Miss Sparks's red dippy bird.

The dippy bird, having been pushed just two inches to the right, jerked its head toward an old metal desk fan, and pushed the button to set it on High.

The fan blew air *up up up,* seven, eight, nine feet in the sky, until it reached the pages of Francine's father's sketchbook, sitting open on a perch near the top of the platform.

The pages fluttered for a moment, then snapped closed, pushing out the tennis ball that had been snuggled inside.

The tennis ball rolled down a small ramp, until it reached the platform where Samson had just finished eating his guinea pig treats.

Samson getting nudged in the butt with the tennis ball was his signal to move again. He crawled up a second ramp to another tilty platform, where there was an open granola bar waiting for him to munch on.

When Samson snagged the granola bar from the platform, the platform tipped, sending a bouquet of flowers smashing into the nearby unicycle.

The unicycle was hung by its seat in such a way that it could *roll roll roll* down another short platform. And attached to the bottom of its wheel was an upside-down hammer. Glued to that hammer was a plastic spoon, whose handle had been sharpened just enough so that, as it rolled along with the unicycle, it could—*SPLAT!*

Ram right through the side of the milk carton.

The milk poured out of the carton, down like a streaming white waterfall to where Francine stood, waiting to catch it with her plastic cup.

When the glass was completely filled up, Francine took an enormous gulp, wiped her mouth with the back of her hand, and smiled.

"See?" Kansas said to the audience. "I told you I could do it. Wasn't that a piece of cake?"

The audience went wild.

29.

An empty plastic cup

Technically, there were still four more acts to go before the talent show was over and the judges announced the winner, but as far as the members of the Media Club were concerned, there wasn't any doubt about who would win. Natalie, Emma, Alicia, and Luis rushed backstage as soon as Francine and Kansas had finished their act, squealing and hugging and shrieking. They made so much noise, in fact, that the stage manager forced them all outside until they could "cool their jets." So there they stood, huddled up together in the teachers' parking lot, pounding their toes against the pavement for warmth and making as much noise as they liked.

Brendan and Andre were outside too, but they weren't

doing any hugging and shrieking. They were mostly sulking over by the garbage cans, whispering to each other and shooting the rest of the group angry looks. With his black cape, Francine thought, Brendan looked rather like a supervillain.

"You did it!" Natalie squealed. "You guys totally did it, I *know* you did. There wasn't anything as good as that crazy machine. Did you *see* Samson when he grabbed that granola bar? Everyone *loved* it. We'll get the money for sure!"

"Ooh, don't say that yet," Emma warned, her hands balled up inside the sleeves of her sweater. Her breath came out in puffs as she spoke. "What if it doesn't come true now 'cause you just said that? Better knock on mud."

"What?" Luis asked.

"She means knock on wood," Alicia explained.

"Yeah," Emma replied. "Wood. Right."

Francine twisted the empty plastic cup from their talent show act in her hands, watching the tiny trail of milk curl around the bottom. As cold as she was, she was pretty sure she had never felt happier.

"So," Luis said, "I guess if you guys really do win the talent show, then you'll *both* be news anchors, right?" Francine looked at Kansas, and Kansas looked at her, but neither of them said anything. "Because you're tied?" Luis went on. "Nine to nine, I think."

"That would be *awesome*," Emma said, "both you guys doing the announcements."

"Yeah," Alicia agreed. "I heard you guys were really funny last week."

As the rest of the group jabbered on and on about how great Media Club would be with Kansas and Francine as co-anchors, Francine stayed silent. So this was it, she thought. After all her hard work, she'd be stuck next to Kansas Bloom after all.

Well, it could have been worse. Maybe, with Kansas next to her, she'd be able to get over her stage fright. Maybe, one day, she'd actually feel as comfortable in front of the camera as she did behind it.

When Francine looked up, she saw Kansas watching her.

"What?" she said.

Kansas stuck his hands deep in his pockets. "You should do it," he told her. His voice was so low that Francine didn't think anyone else had heard him. "News anchor, I mean. You should do it by yourself."

"What?" Francine squinted at him. "But you're so good at it. Calm and . . ." He must have been joking, but he didn't look like he was. He looked dead serious.

"I never really wanted to do it," Kansas said softly. "I thought it should be you from the beginning. That's why I voted for you."

"You *what*? Why would you do that?" The other members of the Media Club were still gabbing, their voices rising and falling, carrying out into the crisp winter air, but Francine's mind was reeling.

Kansas shrugged. "You were the hardest worker in the club, I could tell from the first day."

Francine's mouth dropped open. "But I thought . . ." So it hadn't been Emma or Alicia as her third vote. They'd both picked Kansas. It had been *him*. And she'd paid him back by trying to wallop him with dares.

"So *here's* where you all went off to!"

The members of the Media Club hushed when they realized that Miss Sparks had come outside to join them. Brendan and Andre joined them too, although it looked like they were still brooding.

"I wanted to give everyone the good news," Miss Sparks told them.

"News?" Natalie asked, shooting up on her tiptoes. "What news?"

Their teacher's smile grew broader than Francine had ever seen it. "Kansas and Francine's act won. Can you believe it? A near-unanimous decision. Four votes to one."

"We *won*?" Emma squealed. "We get the money?"

"New camera!" Luis cried. And the cheering started all over again.

But not everyone was happy.

"You've got to be kidding me!" Brendan cried. "That's such a— What a load of— I *quit*!" And before anyone had a chance to say anything about it, Brendan had stormed off into the gym, his black cape swishing behind him.

Andre looked around him for a few seconds, not quite sure what to do. Then, slowly, he made up his mind.

"Yeah," he told them all. "I quit too!" And he turned and followed Brendan back to the gym.

"Well," Miss Sparks said, "that was unfortunate." But no one else seemed to mind too much.

"I wonder which one of the judges didn't vote for you," Alicia said. "You'd have to be *nuts* not to pick you guys."

Francine didn't wonder. Apparently neither did Kansas. "*Mrs. Weinmore,*" they said together. They both laughed.

"It's amazing, really," Miss Sparks said, "and I can't thank you all enough for pulling this off. We'll have a brand-new camera when we get back from winter break, and the club will be better than ever." Francine and the others roared in agreement. "I wonder, though," she went on, "did we ever settle on who was going to be the news anchor next semester?"

Luis was the one to pipe up first. "I think Francine and Kansas are going to split it," he told Miss Sparks. "They can be co-anchors."

"That sounds like a great idea," Miss Sparks said. "Francine and Kansas, what do you think?"

Kansas shrugged. "Maybe it should just be Francine," he said. "That would be fine with me."

The other club members looked surprised at that, but Miss Sparks just nodded. "Francine?" she said. "Do you still want the job?"

Francine tucked a strand of hair—now just the faintest twinge of green—behind her ear. "Maybe we should take another vote," she said. "Just to be sure. I want to make sure it's fair."

"Of course," Miss Sparks replied.

Next to Francine, Natalie reached over and squeezed her hand. Francine looked at her. *This is it,* Natalie's eyes were saying. *You're going to win this time, I know it.*

Francine shot her a message back, with her eyes. And because they'd been best friends since baby daycare, Francine was sure Natalie understood what she was thinking.

"You sure?" Natalie whispered.

Francine nodded.

"Okay," Miss Sparks said. "Let's do a show of hands. All in favor of Francine as our news anchor next semester?"

Francine was sure that Miss Sparks expected everyone

to raise their hands at that. Kansas, too. But news travels fast in the fourth grade, and before Miss Sparks could even get the question out, Natalie had whispered to Emma, who had whispered to Alicia, who had whispered to Luis. And none of them had raised their hands.

Kansas was the only one.

"Huh?" he said, lowering his hand as he looked around him.

"We think you should do it," Francine told him with a smile. "All by yourself."

"Huh?" Kansas said again.

Maybe being news anchor had been her plan from the beginning, Francine figured, but sometimes things didn't go the way you planned them. And sometimes that was the very best thing that could happen.

"You deserve it," she told Kansas. "You're really good at it, and anyway, it turns out I kind of miss being camera-woman."

"But—"

"All in favor?" Miss Sparks asked.

That time all the hands went up—all except Kansas's.

"Well," Miss Sparks said, "I guess that's it, then. Five to one. Congratulations, Kansas."

"B-but"—Kansas stuttered—"but I . . . Francine should really . . . But you've wanted to be news anchor *forever.*"

At that, Francine shrugged. "I guess I just found a new way to be happy," she said.

And she turned, smiling a warm little smile to herself, and walked back toward the gym door to find her parents.

30. A PIECE OF CAKE

Kansas's mother had changed shifts at the gift shop so that she could go to what Ginny was now calling "Mommy and Me and Mrs. Muñoz Yoga." Which meant that when she dropped Kansas off at Luis's birthday party on Sunday, he was a little early.

Well, two hours early.

"Hey, Kansas!" Luis greeted him at the door. "Thanks for coming early to help decorate. Here, put these on." He handed Kansas a pair of Hulk hands, two giant green foam fists, and Kansas slipped them on. Luis had a pair of his own. "Smash, Hulk, smash!" he cried, jabbing Kansas with them.

Kansas laughed. "How're we supposed to decorate with these on?" Each of the hands was as big as his head.

Luis just shrugged. "Well, really my mom's doing most of it because she's afraid I'll mess stuff up. She told us to stay out of her hair. She's kind of freaking out, actually."

"How do you freak out about a birthday party?" Kansas asked.

"You'll see. Come on, I want to show you my room." And Luis led Kansas down the hallway, smashing him with his Hulk fists the whole way.

"Oh, I almost forgot," Luis said when they got to his bedroom. It was full of more comic book stuff than Kansas had ever seen in his life—Wolverine action figures climbing up the bookshelf, Spider-Man posters stuck to the walls, and a menacing Green Goblin hanging from the ceiling. Kansas could already tell he was going to be coming over to Luis's house a *lot*. "Here." Luis thrust a yellow envelope at him.

Kansas stuck one Hulk hand under his armpit and yanked it off, then took the envelope from Luis. "What's this?"

"The photos I took. Of all your dares." Luis sat down on the bed, and Kansas sat next to him, pulling out the pictures. "Some of them are pretty awesome."

Kansas looked. There he was, utterly and totally freaked out in Ginny's tutu, standing in front of the class next to Miss Sparks and a green-haired Francine. In the next picture he was sitting at the lunch table, his chin tilted toward the sky as he howled like a wolf. Kansas grinned as he flipped through them. All the dares were there—the volleyball tryouts, the ice cube on his arm. There was even a photo of him, blurry and spinning, on his first day as news anchor, just as he began to puke.

"These are really good," he told Luis. He tucked the photos back into the envelope.

"If you want," Luis told him, "I'll be your professional photographer. Any more dares you do, you just let me know."

"Thanks," Kansas replied. "But I think I might be done with dares for a while." After all, he thought, he had an image to maintain now. He was Media Club's new announcer, starting in just two weeks—and, much to his surprise, he was actually looking forward to it.

"Boys!" There was a call from the hallway. "Boys?" Luis's mom poked her head inside the room. "I need your help."

From the bed, Luis perked his head up. "Yeah?"

"Well, the bakery dropped off your birthday cake," she explained, "and it's not exactly . . . what I asked for."

"What do you mean?" Luis asked. "They did something wrong?"

"Mmmm . . ." Luis's mother pressed her lips together. "Let's just say that I ordered a vanilla Spider-Man cake with chocolate frosting that says 'Happy Birthday, Luis' on it . . ."

"Yeah?"

"And I got a chocolate *spider* cake with *vanilla* frosting that says 'Happy Birthday, *Luisa*' on it."

Luis snorted. "There's spiders on it?"

"Crawling out of the cake like they're trying to escape the exterminator."

"Cool!" Luis cried. He looked at Kansas, and Kansas laughed.

"It is *not* cool," his mother replied. "It's not what I— Anyway, they're going to bring us a new one."

"Okay," Luis said. "What should we do to help?"

His mother tapped her chin. *"Well,"* she said, her serious look turning into a smile, "I thought you and Kansas might like to help get rid of the first one."

Kansas looked at Luis. Was his mom saying what he thought she was saying?

"You mean," Luis said slowly, "you want us to eat the cake?"

She laughed. "That's what I was thinking. Wouldn't want it to go to waste. After all, it's"—she looked at her watch—"nine thirty in the morning."

Luis rocketed up off the bed. "That sounds like cake-eating time to me! What do you think, Kansas?"

Kansas grinned. "Sounds good, Luisa!" And they raced down the hall.

"Hey," Kansas said when they were sitting at the table, two tall glasses of milk and an entire cake laid out before them. It was absolutely *crawling* with black frosting spiders. "I was thinking." He picked up a fork and dug into the creamy white frosting. *Delicious.* "You should come over to my house next week and play basketball."

288

Luis was already on his fourth bite, his lips speckled with chocolate cake crumbs. "Sure," he said. "Except I kinda stink at it."

"You can be on Mr. Muñoz's team. He keeps trying to play me, and he needs *help*."

"Cool," Luis replied. He shoveled down more cake. "I'm glad you could come to my party. I mean, I'm sorry you couldn't go camping, but . . ."

"I'm not," Kansas said. And as soon as the words came out of his mouth, he knew they were true. He wasn't mad at Ricky and Will anymore, he realized, not really. If they wanted to be friends with him again, that would be fine. But in the meantime, he had plenty of friends right here in California.

It had taken him a while to realize it, Kansas thought as he chugged down a gulp of milk, but Ginny had been wrong, that day in the hospital. *We don't need anybody,* that's what she'd said. And at the time, Kansas had agreed. But it turned out that Kansas *did* need people.

It just wasn't always the ones he'd expected.

"Hey," Luis said suddenly, "I bet you can't eat this

entire piece of cake right here"—he motioned with his fork—"before I can eat *this* part."

Kansas raised an eyebrow. It was a *very* large piece of cake, about as big as his hand. He took a long swig of milk and thought about it. "I bet I can," he said, setting his glass down with a thunk.

"Oh, yeah?" A smile stretched across Luis's face. "I double dog dare you."